BACK TO POMPEII

A TIME TRAVEL ROMANCE

LOVE THROUGHOUT TIME
BOOK THIRTEEN

ID JOHNSON

For Lisa. Thanks for being so good.

CONTENTS

 1. Believe — 1
 2. Logistics — 9
 3. Tempus et Fatum — 15
 4. Preparations — 23
 5. Dreaming — 29
 6. Alluring — 37
 7. Fortuna — 43
 8. Opportunity — 51
 9. Destiny — 59
10. Complicated — 67
11. Envy and Regret — 75
12. Gladiators — 83
13. What He's Missing — 91
14. Retribution — 99
15. Courageous — 107
16. Word Spreads — 115
17. Electricity — 123
18. Plans — 129
19. Falling — 137
20. Miracle — 143
21. Warning! — 151
22. Life and Death — 157
23. The Woman Who Saved Pompeii — 165
24. By the Gods — 173

Also by ID Johnson — 177

1

BELIEVE

FIONA

Excitement for tonight's ceremony and the award I will be accepting for my work on the Puebloan ruins has fueled me all week. Stepping into the dimly lit ballroom, the orchestra playing, the well-dressed audience around me, and the surge of adrenaline that comes every time I think of my acceptance speech is overwhelming in the best way. I take my seat near the front next to my colleagues as the lights flicker, signaling that the ceremony is about to begin.

From her seat beside me, Dr. Moreno leans over and smiles. "Fiona, the way you reconstructed the Puebloan site layouts from those fragmentary ruins was brilliant. You really made their village come alive. You deserve this award tonight."

"Thank you, that means a lot coming from you, Sandy," I reply. "I'm proud of what we all accomplished, and it's wonderful to see it recognized. I just hope I'm not so nervous that I start to ramble up there."

"Don't be nervous," she says softly. "You're always articulate and entertaining. You'll do great."

"I appreciate that," I whisper as the lights dim further, and a hush spreads through the room. The orchestra softens, and the host steps onto the stage.

I scan the seats around me, recognizing archaeologists, surveyors, consultants, lab technicians, and historians. They're friendly, but none of them are family or close friends. I moved to Santa Fe not long ago, and I don't have anyone here beyond these acquaintances, so this award feels like a lift for my spirit.

The first award is announced, and the audience applauds as a peer I've only ever seen in panels, Regina Green, stands. Her husband rises with her and kisses her on the cheek before she walks up onto the stage to accept her award.

As Regina begins her acceptance speech, I notice a couple of children sitting near her husband, and a twinge of sadness mixes with a vague sense of jealousy. Maybe someday the audience will hold someone for me, but even when I won awards at school as a teenager, my family wasn't there. My grandmother took over raising me after my parents died in a car accident when I was twelve. She worked constantly, so she was rarely able to attend school events.

Regina gives a brief acceptance speech, and I clap, genuinely happy for her, as the ceremony continues. One after another, awards are given. Speeches offer thanks and acknowledgments, and I drift in and out of listening, my mind rehearsing what I'll say when it's my turn. The feeling grows, a tightening of nerves and anticipation. Tonight is about recognition and affirmation, a reminder that I can be proud of the work I've done here.

The host says, "And now, for her contributions to the study of Puebloan ruins... Fiona Lockwood."

Applause fills the auditorium as I stand and walk to the stage in the sapphire gown I chose for tonight, a color that brings out my blue eyes.

I begin my acceptance speech. "When I was a little girl, my father and I would watch Indiana Jones over and over." I smile as the audience chuckles, because I'm sure everyone in this room can relate.

"He always told me that I could be anything I wanted when I grew up. When I was twelve, he and my mother passed away in a car accident, and for a little while, my ability to dream and to believe that I could be anything I wanted vanished. But tonight, when I look out at all of your faces, the faces of such respected and unbelievably gifted archaeologists, I know my dad was right. We can all achieve our dreams. We just have to believe in ourselves. Thank you."

Toward the end of my speech, I start to feel a little sentimental and pretentious, especially since most people accepting awards tonight are just getting up and saying a quick thank you. But by the time I finish, people are rising for a standing ovation.

I make my way back to my seat with the trophy in my hands, still beaming with pride and buzzing with adrenaline. I never expected the crowd to react with such enthusiasm.

The ceremony continues, and soon, we reach the final speeches. As the last few words are spoken, the orchestra music swells again, signaling the end. The energy in the room rises as people begin to prepare for the next part of the evening.

Guests stand and make their way toward the ballroom. I follow the crowd, stepping into the room as the scent of fresh flowers and savory dishes fills the air. The sound of a jazz band greets me, setting the tone for the evening. People sip champagne and chat as the atmosphere shifts. Some move toward the dance floor; others order their dinner from menus at each place setting.

I wander around until I spot my name on a card at one of the stunningly decorated tables. Cream and coral flowers are arranged beautifully, and tiny archaeology tool decorations add a playful yet elegant touch.

I pull out my chair and take a seat, still unsure if I'm hungry or too nervous to eat. A waiter passes by with a tray of champagne, and I raise my finger to signal him. He brings me a glass and I take a sip. It's the deliciously expensive kind. I look around the room, wishing I had someone to share this moment with.

As I sit there, lost in thought, a tall man in a well-tailored suit approaches with a warm smile. "Miss Hammer, do you mind if I sit?" he asks.

I gesture to the empty chair next to mine. "Please."

"I just wanted to congratulate you on your award," he says, sitting down. "And your speech was incredibly moving, but it's your work I'm most impressed by."

I can't help but smile. "Thank you. I'm sorry, have we had the pleasure of—"

He jumps in. "Oh, where are my manners?" He offers his hand, and I shake it. "I'm James Delacroix. I work on an archaeological team that's looking for someone with your expertise and enthusiasm. I also heard through the grapevine that you're fluent in Greek and Latin, as well as an expert in ancient Roman history. Is that true?"

"Yes, that's true," I say, smiling. "You didn't just read it off my LinkedIn, did you?"

He laughs. "No, but actually, I do want to offer you what I feel is the opportunity of a lifetime."

My mind skips from Delphi to Olympia, then from Knossos to Mycenae, and even to Ostia Antica, each possibility flashing through quickly as I try to guess what he's about to say.

"We're looking for someone to join our dig in Pompeii," he continues, a gleam of excitement in his eyes.

I'm glad I'm not sipping my champagne. I would've spit it all over him. "Pompeii?" I ask, astonished. "You can't be serious."

He nods, smiling mischievously. "Of course I am. There are three topics I never joke about: death, taxes, and Pompeii."

"I'm in. When do we leave?"

He chuckles. "I was hoping you'd say that. We leave at the end of the month. I'll get with you about all the details on Monday morning. I'm glad you'll be joining our team, Fiona."

We pull out our phones and exchange numbers. "Thank you so much for this opportunity," I say as we rise and shake hands once more in parting.

"It was nice meeting you, Fiona. I look forward to working with you."

"It was nice meeting you as well," I reply.

"I'm going to go mingle," he says with a grin and walks off.

I sit back down, letting it sink in. This is the kind of opportunity

I've worked toward for years, the chance to apply everything I've learned in the field. The award tonight was recognition of my work, but this invitation feels like a step into the future I've been striving for. Every late night in the archives, every long excavation, every challenge I've faced, every hour I spent learning Greek and Latin, mastering how to read their graffiti and pronounce their ancient dialects, will all pay off now. I feel satisfaction knowing that my skills, knowledge, and dedication are valued and needed.

The rest of the evening passes in a blur of laughter and extravagant dishes, which I taste and appreciate even as my mind drifts back to Pompeii. A few coworkers and acquaintances ask me to dance, and I oblige politely, raising my glass to a couple of toasts in between.

Later, as I ride home in a cab, I can't stop thinking about the dig. We're not leaving until the end of the month, but I'm already imagining what I'll need to pack and how I'll prepare for the most epic adventure of my entire career.

A MONTH OF CAREFUL PLANNING AND PREPARATION HAS PASSED. I organize my gear meticulously: notebooks, trowels, brushes, measuring instruments. Every item has its place in my case. I review excavation plans and site maps, running through each area in my head. I imagine the first steps I'll take on the streets of Pompeii, picturing the fragments and inscriptions waiting to be uncovered.

Finally, the day arrives. The plane lifts off smoothly, carrying the team to Italy. James sits beside me, flipping through his notes, and after a while, he looks over at me. "How did you learn Latin and Greek well enough to read and speak fluently?"

"Years of reading whatever I could get my hands on. I read inscriptions, religious and ancient texts wherever I could find them. I practiced pronunciation, translated in context, and worked with experts. Knowing the languages isn't just about the words; it's about understanding the culture, daily life, and how people expressed themselves."

He nods. "That kind of expertise is rare."

"It helps me notice details others might miss," I say. "Every symbol tells a story. Understanding the language is how you learn the people."

The conversation drifts to logistics and schedules, and I review plans in my head, thinking about which sections we'll tackle first. I picture trowels brushing ash and dust away, fragments of walls revealed, inscriptions coming to light.

After layovers, changing flights, and a long overnight in the air, we finally arrive in Italy. I'm exhausted, but the sight of the coastline and the distant ruins on the drive south sharpens my focus. A shuttle carries the team through hills dotted with villas and past the sprawling site until we reach our hotel in modern Pompeii's town center, just minutes from the entrance to the ruins.

Once I'm in my room, I close the door behind me, drop my bag on the floor, walk over to the balcony door, and push it open. From here, I can see the bright green leaves and yellow lemons of the trees lining the street below, and the faint scent of citrus drifts up, mingling with the rich aroma of coffee from a nearby café. The distant hum of conversation and the occasional clatter of dishes reach me, blending with the soft rustle of leaves in the breeze.

I step back into the room and flop onto the bed, letting myself stretch out fully. Sunlight streams through tall windows, illuminating pale stone walls and casting shadows across the terra-cotta tiles. The room is larger than I expected, with a high ceiling. The furniture is minimal but elegant, and a few touches of local craftsmanship—a woven rug, hand-painted ceramics—give it character. I'm glad it's beautiful because I'll be staying here for the next few weeks, living and working beside the ruins, and it feels like a place where I can actually breathe.

I take a short nap, just long enough to shake off the travel fatigue. Later, I join the team for our evening meal. The table is filled with fresh garlic bread, glasses of rich red wine, and laughter that drifts through the room. We listen to the people around us speaking Italian and revel in being somewhere so ancient and yet completely new to us.

After dinner, we walk back to our hotel under the glow of the streetlights. A shiver runs up my spine at the thought of how close we are to the ruins of Pompeii.

Back in my room, I change into something comfortable, brush my teeth, run through my skincare routine, and slide under the covers, thinking about the dig waiting for me at first light. These relics have held their secrets for centuries, and now, I'll be part of uncovering them.

2

——————————

LOGISTICS

MARCUS

I step into the market forum, morning light brightening the stalls. Quintus is already there, looking over a ledger as he watches the merchants set up their tables. "We have a tight squeeze near the north gate," he says, gesturing toward a row of fruit sellers. "The crowd will get stuck there if we don't shift a few tables."

I nod. "Good catch. Move the wine vendors three spaces south and stagger the vegetable stalls. That should open a small corridor for people to pass without crushing each other."

Quintus scribbles quickly. "And the wool merchants? They're on the west side. If the crowd spills from the west gate, they'll block access to the temple steps."

"Right," I murmur. "Shift them closer to the center. Leave the steps clear for offerings to Jupiter. We don't want anyone stumbling on holy ground."

A merchant with a bundle of figs approaches, bowing low. "Praetor Marcus, will the placement of my stall near the eastern entrance be suitable?"

I consider the arrangement. "It will, but please keep out of the walkway and mark your prices clearly. Confusion slows traffic."

The man nods and scurries off.

Quintus leans close, whispering, "The dancers' space near the fountain might be too small. They'll knock over the wine barrels."

I glance over. "Ah, yes. We'll move the dancers toward the south end. Keeping them near the Temple of Venus is more proper for honoring her during the Vinalia Rustica. That also gives the wine sellers more prominence. People will see them before the feasting begins."

A young scribe with a ledger of his own hurries over. "Praetor Marcus, the amphorae suppliers requested extra space near the central square. They say the last festival's traffic blocked their wagons."

I straighten and wave toward Quintus. "Note it. We'll allocate them two additional spaces, but mark the boundary clearly. I don't want carts tipping over and causing anyone to get hurt."

Quintus grins. "You're the greatest with logistics, Marcus."

"I'm trying to prevent chaos," I reply, smiling. "Even Jupiter appreciates order, or so I hope."

We walk the stalls again, checking labels, measuring spaces, and imagining the flow of the crowd.

Quintus gestures toward the empty area near the southern edge of the forum. "We'll need a pen for the livestock here, or they'll be in the way once they arrive."

"Yes," I say. "Mark the space clearly, and keep the fragile goods well away."

By midday, we pause in the forum, taking in the space. Empty tables line the stone square, each marked for grapes, wine, fabric, and other goods. Brightly colored banners flap from the colonnades, and the space for offerings at the Temple of Jupiter, honoring the triad of Jupiter, Juno, and Minerva, stands prepared for the festival. We have a few last-minute changes to make, but for the most part, everything is arranged and ready, waiting for the merchants, livestock, and townspeople to bring it to life.

Quintus leans over to me. "This will be remembered as one of the best Vinalia Rustica preparations in years."

I allow myself a smile, glancing at the city streets flowing with life. "Yes," I say, "but only if the gods enjoy it as much as the people do."

After spending most of the afternoon working with the builders putting up the livestock pens and coordinating with the farmers and shepherds, we step back into the shade. "Quintus, we're done for today," I say. "The forum is in order, but we'll be making more adjustments over the next few days before the festival."

He gives a quick smile. "Looks like a good stopping point for now."

"Yes," I reply. "Go home, say hello to your family for me, have a meal, and rest. Tomorrow, we pick up where we left off."

"I'll do that," he says with a small smile. "Have a good evening, Marcus."

Quintus waves and heads off, and I turn toward my parents' house, leaving the forum behind for the day. The noise of merchants and animals fades as I walk, the familiar path winding past stone and brick houses on narrow lanes. I pass a group of children carrying buckets from a nearby well and nod to an elderly woman tending her small garden. The city moves around me, alive with a rhythm I've known my whole life.

I walk up the stone path to my parents' house. Just as I reach the door, the faint clatter of hammer on metal reaches me from the workshop beside the house. Curious, I walk over and push open the door.

Inside, Lucius is bent over his workbench, heating a bronze bowl in a brazier and shaping it with careful strikes. Sparks leap with each strike, and he wipes sweat from his brow.

"Marcus," he calls, straightening. "You're earlier than usual."

"I finished work for today," I reply, setting down my satchel. "How's it coming?"

He holds up the bowl. "Master Antonius says my strikes are more precise than yesterday but that I still have a lot to learn."

I smile, stepping closer. "Precision is earned, Lucius. Keep your wrist steady, and plan every move before striking. That lesson applies to more than metalwork."

There is a soft knock at the workshop door, and Lucius looks up from his work and says, "Enter."

A servant girl, Lydia, steps inside and bows. "Master Marcus, Master Lucius, dinner is served," she says politely.

"Thank you, Lydia," I reply.

We follow her into the house and take our seats at the table, where our mother and father are already waiting.

"What's on the menu today?" I ask Mother, leaning over to kiss her cheek.

"Nothing extravagant," she says, smiling. "Bread, olives, cheese, and lamb."

"Sounds delicious," Lucius says. "I'm starving."

My father looks up from the plate Lydia has just placed before him. "Thank you, Lydia." Then, turning to me, he asks, "Are the festival preparations going smoothly?"

"Yes," I reply. "Tables are in place, pens set, banners hung. Everything is coming together, but there's plenty of work left for the coming days."

He nods, eyes twinkling. "Good. You always think of everything. We're proud to see you taking care of it all."

Mother leans forward, eager. "Tell me more about the festival layout and the schedule of events."

I describe the rows of tables and the offerings at the temple, the dancing, jugglers, and worship singers, gesturing as I speak. "Each space is planned so that everything flows, and everyone can move freely. Hopefully, everyone has a pleasant time."

"It sounds like you have everything well in hand. I imagine it will be quite a sight once everyone arrives," Mother says.

Lucius grins. "And I suppose you'll make sure there's plenty of room for everyone to move freely without anyone getting injured like last year."

"I will try," I say, sighing. "No promises." Last year, a bottleneck nearly cost a friend his leg when someone tripped in front of him, and he got trampled. I will not let it happen again.

We talk a little longer about Lucius's practice in the workshop and

Mother's household matters. Laughter rises easily between the four of us as we share memories of past festivals.

Mother shares a story of when Lucius was four and I was nine. He'd gotten away from her. We frantically searched all around the festival grounds for him, finally finding him in the fountain, swimming while the dancers performed around him.

Father laughs and recalls the time I insisted on eating a plate of honeyed figs, promising I wouldn't make a mess—and yet, we had to leave early because I ended up covered head to toe in the sticky, sweet fruit.

"In my defense, I was only seven," I remind him.

"Yes, you were only seven," Mother replies, smiling, "but you were covered in tufts of wool from all the sheep you insisted on petting with sticky hands, Marcus."

Her comment earns the biggest laugh of the evening, and by the time we finish, Lydia has cleared the dishes, and we're on our third glass of wine each. When I finally rise, it's dusk. "Thank you for the meal. It was good to eat together."

Mother smiles warmly. "You're always welcome here, Marcus. Don't let the city or the festival keep you from your family."

"Oh, Mother, I would never do that," I say. "I'll most likely see you all tomorrow. Until then, good night."

Lucius stands and walks me to the door, placing a hand on my shoulder. "Marcus, if you need any help with the festival plans, let me know."

"I appreciate that, brother," I reply.

He nods, and I step outside, closing the door behind me and making my way toward home.

As I walk, I think of Lucius. He's a good young man, though he used to get into trouble quite a bit. I hope those days are behind him and that he continues to grow into a capable nobleman.

By the time I reach home, I'm exhausted. I push the door open and step inside. It's quiet, the soft glow of a lamp casting long shadows along the walls. I sink into a chair, and my dog, Felix, lean and wolf-like, pads over and rests at my feet. I reach down and run a hand over his back.

One of my servants, Aurelia, enters the room, holding a tray with a glass of wine and some cheese. She sets it carefully on the table in front of me. "For you, before you rest, sir."

I nod. "Thank you. You and the others are dismissed for the evening."

She bows and leaves the room.

As I sip my wine, Felix gets up, undoubtedly to look for his ball, as he does every evening. When he finds it, he brings it over to me. I take it, tossing it across the room, and he bolts after it. He brings it back, tail wagging. I throw it once more, and lean back in my chair, letting the quiet settle around me. My life is good. I have important work that helps people in my community, and I enjoy it most of the time. I have incredibly loyal friends like Quintus, whom I trust, and a family I care for… but I don't have a wife yet. I imagine meeting someone worth sharing this life with, but tonight, like every other night, that fantasy feels out of reach.

3

TEMPUS ET FATUM

My team and I climb into a van as a gorgeous sunrise spreads over the horizon. When we arrive at the site for the first time, I can't help but stop and stare, breathless. I've only ever dreamt about this place, and no photographs or textbooks could have prepared me for actually standing here.

Trying to keep up with the others and take everything in is impossible. It's like time was frozen for centuries in the streets, the worn grooves from cart wheels, the faded frescoes clinging stubbornly to plaster. All around me, I see the delicate imprint of lives ended far too quickly.

The project leader, James Delacroix, gathers us near a partially exposed structure and runs through the plan for the day, explaining each step clearly. I appreciate that he doesn't waste time. We're assigned sections, and I gather my tool bag and follow the path James has marked, scanning the grid until I find the square assigned to me.

When I get to my spot, I excitedly pull my trowel from my bag and kneel at my assigned square, tunnel vision forming as everything else slips away, and I focus on the ash and dust beneath me. The noise from the crew fades. It's just me, the earth, and whatever history is waiting underneath.

Each brushstroke, every careful scrape, reminds me of how lucky I am to be here. I remember the first time I saw the bodies posed in a snapshot of time. It was in a *Weekly Reader* in fourth grade social studies class, and I was fascinated, imagining what it would be like to explore a place like this. And now, out of everyone in the world who felt the same way, I'm actually here. I get to touch the halted existence of this place and uncover lives entombed, suspended in time, with my own hands.

Time goes by too quickly, and by midmorning, I'm uncovering a small fragment—pottery, by the look of it, but not like the examples we have studied. The edge is unusually fine, and the pigment is much darker, almost metallic beneath the dust. When I notice the subtle differences in texture and material, I pause, my pulse kicking up, and signal for James.

He kneels beside me, studying it without touching. "Good eye," he says finally, and that's enough to send a quiet spark of pride through me. Hours later, the partial vase is lifted properly, logged, and documented, but I can't stop thinking about the remarkable artifact. Who held it? What was it used for? And how did it end up here, in this exact location?

By the time the sun begins to set, and we pack up, my muscles ache, and my hands are dirty in a way that feels earned. I'm tired, but it's the kind of satisfying exhaustion that comes with doing work I truly love. Heading toward the van, the day's duties done, I keep looking back, drawn to every stone and shadow, to the traces of life buried here. I want to keep digging, keep uncovering, but the sun is getting lower, and I can't work after dark.

The crew climbs into the van, our gear packed in the back, and we return to the hotel as the city drifts past in the golden evening light.

When the van pulls up to the hotel, we all hop out and grab our tool bags from the back. Another archaeologist, Jackie, catches up to me in the lobby, beaming. "Can you believe how much we uncovered today?"

"I know," I reply, swinging my bag over my shoulder. "I didn't expect the work to feel so intimate on the first day."

"I was watching you at your square when you found that vase," she says. "You were in the zone. I thought I was impressed with the coin I found, but you—wow."

I laugh, shaking my head. "You found a coin? That's amazing! I can't wait to see it tomorrow."

We turn down the hall toward our rooms, which are side-by-side. "And I can't wait to see the pottery you uncovered. Do you think we'll hit something even bigger tomorrow?" she asks.

"I hope so." I smile at the thought. "I can't stop thinking about how we are only at surface level. There's so much we didn't even get to today."

Her smile widens. "Yeah, we barely scratched the top level. It's going to be an amazing journey. It feels like we stepped into a time machine."

We reach our rooms, and Jackie unlocks hers. Before stepping inside, she says, "I'm starving. See you at dinner?"

"Absolutely," I answer. She nods, slips inside her room, and I unlock mine and step in. I close the door behind me, still buzzing from the site and already thinking ahead to tomorrow.

I set my bag down and peel off my dusty clothes, running a hot shower and letting the water wash away the grime clinging to my skin. The hotel's fancy orange blossom shampoo and conditioner fill the air with a sweet, citrus scent as I lather up. When I step out, I twist my damp hair into a clip and step into a sea-green dress with lacy straps, something easy to move in but still nice enough for dinner. Once I'm dressed, I unclip my hair and style it in loose curls, then finish with a touch of subtle makeup before heading to the lobby to meet up with my co-workers.

One by one, they emerge from the stairs, and we walk down the street to the small trattoria nearby. Inside, the incredible smells of garlic, tomato, and fresh bread hit me, mingling with the chatter of locals around us. The second we're seated, conversations immediately explode among the team.

"I didn't expect to find a foreign coin at that layer," Jackie says, shaking her head. "I can't wait to figure out where it came from. It's definitely not from this region."

Kyle, the assistant field director who helps oversee the dig and guide the team's work, sets his wineglass down. "If we get enough artifacts from other regions, maybe we can secure a grant to visit sites in other areas, as well."

Eliza beams. "That would be epic!" I've known Eliza since before my work on the Pueblo site, and she's always been ready for the next challenge.

Our director, James, raises his glass. "We made a lot of progress today, everyone. Good work. To tomorrow."

"To tomorrow," we all repeat, clinking our glasses and taking a sip.

With everyone so enthusiastic after only our first day, I feel my excitement growing. Then Eliza turns to me. "What about you, Fiona? Find anything interesting on your first day?"

"I did. Why don't I sketch out what I found?" I pull a small notepad and pen from my bag and sketch the vase's unusual markings. "It has inscriptions in Latin," I explain. "But it's not the kind of Latin the people of Pompeii would have spoken or written. The phrasing is different—more formal and almost poetic. It says 'Tempus et Fatum'—Time and Destiny."

Jackie leans over, her eyes filled with wonder. "Really? That's perfect!"

Kyle tilts his head to look at my sketch. "Yes, eerily so. I've never seen markings like that before. Where exactly did you find it?"

I describe the layer in the ash, the texture under my trowel, and the way the material of the vase felt different. I draw quickly, explaining each detail as questions fly from the others.

As the meal continues, the table vibrates with energy, everyone feeding off the discoveries, the possibilities, and I'm already planning how I'll examine my area more carefully tomorrow. I keep glancing at my sketch, imagining what else might be waiting beneath the dust, and I feel an intensity I haven't felt in years. In Pompeii, I feel so alive, focused, and utterly in my element.

By the time we leave the restaurant, I am both exhausted and exhilarated. This first day has exceeded every expectation, and I can't wait to get back to the site in the morning.

I WAKE BEFORE DAWN, THE HOTEL QUIET EXCEPT FOR THE LOW HUM OF the city waking outside my window. My bag is ready from the night before, so I slip into my clothes and pull my hair back, securing it with a clip before heading to the bathroom to wash my face and brush my teeth. By the time I step into the lobby, the others are gathering near the door.

James spots me and waves. "Ready to get back out there?"

"Absolutely." I catch up to the group.

Jackie is checking her gear. She grins at me. "You look like you've been counting down the minutes."

"Maybe I have," I reply, laughing. My stomach flips with anticipation.

The ride to the site is short, the van bouncing along the old stone roads. Kyle checks the site map spread on his lap. "If we start on the eastern squares first, we might uncover more fragments similar to yesterday's. It looks promising."

"That makes sense. Focusing there could help us understand how the foreign coins and fragments relate to the rest of the site," Eliza says.

Jackie nods. "I can't wait to get out there. Every new find feels like a small door opening."

When we arrive at the dig site for our second day, I drop my bag near my assigned excavation square, pull my padded mat out, and kneel on it. I begin carefully brushing aside tiny shards of debris in the fine, gritty ash when something catches my attention. As I gently use my brush and trowel, a line of bricks comes into view, partially buried and pushed at an odd angle. "What is this?" I murmur under my breath, tracing the edge with my hands.

Slowly, it becomes clear. A section of wall has collapsed here, its shape and position hinting at how the fragments around it were once arranged. Each detail adds to the story I'm piecing together.

Jackie is working next to me, carefully brushing ash from her square. I glance up at her and say, "Jackie, come and look at this. I think I found part of a collapsed wall."

She walks over and crouches beside me. "You're right." She studies the bricks. "This section could tell us if a building used to stand here. If we map it carefully, it might explain the layout of this area."

By midmorning, James joins us at my square. "Fiona, have you made any progress on the origin of that vase you found yesterday?"

"I'm working near the area where I found it and have mapped the immediate surroundings. But no, I haven't made any new discoveries regarding the vase. Jackie and I are working on something even better this morning." I show him our work. "There's a collapsed wall segment here. Debris and ash variations suggest it was positioned between buildings."

He nods in approval. "Interesting. Keep track of everything. This might be the most informative piece of architecture we've seen yet."

I thank him, and Jackie and I return to our work, carefully uncovering the wall little by little.

When it's time for lunch, we sit at a table in a shady spot just outside the site. James's assistant has set out plates of bread, cheese, and cured meats, along with jugs of water and lemonade. Conversation flows easily as we eat, swapping observations from the morning's work.

Jackie gestures with a piece of bread. "They were likely planning a Feriae Augusti festival, or the Vinalia Rustica, at this time, which celebrated Jupiter and Venus and was tied to the grape harvest. Public feasts, temple offerings, and games would have been part of the celebration."

Eliza chimes in. "That would explain why so many decorated vessels are coming from the same area. Festivals would need larger, specialized vessels, maybe even imports."

"And if we tie the fragment markings to festival use, it will most likely align with what we see in Pompeii murals and mosaics," I say.

"The more we find, the clearer the picture becomes. Every fragment adds context," Kyle adds.

After lunch, the day grows even hotter, but I stay focused. Jackie has gone back to her square, and I'm left carefully brushing ash from the collapsed wall, working slowly to expose its full outline. The bricks are uneven, many still partially buried, and I make note of how they've shifted over time. I keep at it, determined to uncover the entire section and understand how it once stood.

I'm so absorbed in my work, completely caught up in the wall's details, that for a moment, nothing else exists. When I step back to get a better view, I misjudge the edge of a trench where another archaeologist has made a huge amount of progress.

The ground falls away beneath me, and I lunge into a deep hollow, hitting my head on a jagged rock. Intense pain rips through my skull. The sounds of the dig fade, distant and muffled, and my vision wavers. I try to call for help, but no sound comes out of my mouth. Weak and dizzy, I try to stand, but darkness pulls me under.

4

PREPARATIONS

Marcus

I wake before dawn, Felix already at my bedside, nudging my hand with his nose. He whines softly, his tail thumping against the wall, insistent on his breakfast. "Good morning, Felix," I murmur, scratching behind his ears. He nudges me again, impatient, and I laugh.

I rise from bed and dress quickly in a simple linen tunica, securing it at the waist with a belt. The warm smell of bread and honey drifts through the domus as I step into the dining room, Felix following at my heels.

Aurelia is arranging the breakfast tray on the table. "Good morning, Dominus Marcus," she says with a bow. "Your breakfast is ready."

"Thank you, Aurelia," I reply.

I sit down at the table as Aurelia sets a small bowl of scraps on the floor for Felix. He sniffs it and digs in.

She bows once again and returns to the kitchen. The soft sounds of other servants moving through the domus reach me—the scrape of brooms, quiet footsteps, faint murmurs as they go about their morning tasks. I finish the last of my bread and figs, glancing out at the sunrise. Work is waiting. I stand, ready to meet it.

"Come on, Felix. You can go with me today. Let's not keep Quintus waiting." I reach down and pat him on the head. The dog follows me to the door. Before we leave, I pick up his ball, tuck it into my pocket, and we set off toward the forum.

We step outside as the streets of Pompeii are waking. Merchants prepare their stalls, and the delicious smells of freshly baked goods drift from nearby bakeries. My dog and I walk through our neighborhood, and I greet friends and acquaintances as we pass.

By the time I arrive at the forum, the square is already alive with activity. Quintus waits near the central platform, a rolled scroll tucked under his arm.

"Good morning, Marcus," he greets me. "All the stalls are still set the way we had them yesterday. Nothing was touched overnight."

"Good morning, Quintus," I reply. "That's great news. We can pick up right where we left off."

He squats down to look Felix in the eye, petting his head. "Are you going to help us today, good boy?" he asks the dog.

"Hopefully, he helps more than he hurts," I mutter with a smirk.

We begin our inspection, moving from the market stalls to the offerings tables. I pause at the altars, studying the flower garlands draped along the pillars. "If the sun hits these flowers too early, they could wilt before the ceremony begins," I say.

Quintus nods, jotting notes on his scroll and carefully adjusting the placement of the decorations to keep them safe from the morning heat.

"We need to go over the schedule of events once more." I scan the list on my scroll. "Make sure each procession, offering, and performance is timed correctly so nothing overlaps. Otherwise, everything seems ready for the Vinalia Rustica."

Quintus nods. "The townspeople are excited. You can feel it in the air."

I pause, looking over the forum, the bustle, the neatly aligned stalls, and the ceremonial spaces prepared to honor Jupiter and Venus filling me with pride. The coordination, the smooth execution, the anticipation of the festival, is the kind of order I value most.

"It's all falling into place," I tell Quintus. "We've done well."

He smiles, folding the scroll under his arm. "It will go well, Marcus. Thanks to your planning."

"I couldn't do any of it without your help." We walk along the forum streets, Felix following closely, and settle at a table near the edge of the forum, unrolling Quintus's scroll between us. I lean over it, tracing the order of events with my finger as I speak. "Jugglers, dancers, musicians, and games after that."

Quintus taps his stylus against the scroll. "Should we move the games to begin before the performers? That might give the crowd time to spread out."

I nod. "That could work. The games will build the excitement leading into the performances."

He taps his chin thoughtfully. "Right. That makes sense."

We continue through the performances, talking over timing and order, making sure nothing will overlap or cause confusion. I'm fully absorbed in coordinating the day while Felix curls up at my feet, lifting his head now and then to glance up at me as if checking if I'm still paying attention to him.

"All right, all right. I see you," I murmur, giving him a quick scratch behind the ear before returning to the schedule.

I hear a commotion from the far side of the forum. I look over and see two merchants arguing over a stall. They're pointing at the tables and shouting, their voices growing louder and angrier with each moment. Quintus and I both rise from the table. Felix lifts his head, ears up, body low and tense, watching the men.

We step closer, keeping our eyes on the merchants making trouble. Both of the men lean forward, their chests pressing toward each other, hands stabbing through the air as they argue. Their words are sharp, cutting through the morning bustle. I can see their anger in their stiff shoulders, tight jaws, and fingers jabbing at each other.

"Enough!" I call, stepping forward. My hand hovers near my belt, brushing the hilt of my sword, a warning in my posture. Both men freeze, blinking at me, their anger colliding with my authority.

Quintus moves up beside me in case anything happens and he needs to back me up.

I glance at the space between the stalls, studying the men, ready to act again if they make a sudden move. "You two will not argue over this space. There's no need," I say firmly. "Shift your stalls back a step. You each get your corner, and no one loses space. Agreed?"

The merchants glare, breathing heavily, but the message seems to reach them. One grumbles, nodding his head and backing off. The other follows. I keep my gaze fixed on them, making sure they understand I mean every word I speak.

Quintus immediately notes the adjustment on the scroll, recording the change in placement exactly as it happens. Felix stays at my feet, the fur on the back of his neck standing on end.

I watch for any signs of renewed argument, but the two men seem to settle down—for now. We step away and walk back through the forum, talking about the preparations once more before realizing it's nearly time for the midday meal.

"Look at that. The sun is already high enough that my stomach should be growling any minute," Quintus says with a chuckle. "Would you like to come to my house for lunch? Felix is welcome, too."

"Thank you, Quintus. That's very generous. I'd be glad to, and I know Felix would. He's always ready for lunch." We head down the street toward Quintus's place.

When we reach the small house, I follow my friend inside, the warm air and the scent of roasted lamb greeting us. Cornelia stands by the hearth, wiping her hands on her apron.

"Marcus! Welcome," she says, smiling. "I hope you haven't had too busy a morning." She then turns to Quintus, placing a kiss on his cheek before pulling him into a warm embrace.

"Not at all," I reply. "The forum is nearly ready for the festival, but I'm glad to take a break." I glance down at my dog. "And Felix seems very glad to be here as well."

Julia, only four, runs in from the backyard, squealing as soon as she spots him. 'Felix! Felix is here!'"

Her two-year-old brother, Gaius, is right behind her, his eyes wide with wonder. "Marcus, can we ride him?"

I can't help but laugh. "He's a dog, not a pony. But you can toss his ball for him." I reach into my pocket and pull out Felix's ball. "Here. Throw it, and he'll go and get it for you." I hand it to Gaius.

He grabs it eagerly, eyes shining, and tosses the ball across the room. Felix chases after it, picks it up, and trots back to Gaius, dropping the ball at his feet. The children shriek with excitement, petting Felix and showering him with praise.

"Be gentle," Cornelia says with a smile. "He's big, but he's not a toy."

"I know!" Julia giggles, hugging Felix's neck. "You're so soft, Felix!"

The dog nudges Gaius gently with his nose, which makes the boy laugh. Julia squeals again, tossing the ball across the floor once more, and the dog brings it back to them immediately.

I laugh and follow Cornelia into the dining room, where Quintus pours wine into small cups for us and sets bread and olives on the table. "I hope you're hungry," he says, gesturing to the food.

"I'm starving," I admit, sliding into a chair. "It smells wonderful, Cornelia."

The children continue to play with Felix in the other room, occasionally racing through the dining room and past the table, giggling. I keep a watchful eye on them, though I can't suppress a smile as the dog patiently indulges every hug and rough pet to the neck.

"Felix is perfect with them," Cornelia says, standing by the hearth. "I'm glad he's so gentle with the children."

"He's a good boy," I agree. "And he's very loyal."

Julia tugs at my sleeve. "Marcus, can he stay with us forever?"

I chuckle. "For now, he lives with me, but I think he enjoys visiting your house."

The children erupt in laughter again as Felix brings back the ball for another round. Quintus and Cornelia exchange amused glances, clearly used to this kind of chaos by now, while I settle in to enjoy the meal and the rare moment of calm before the festival planning resumes.

As I sit at their table, watching my friend and his wife, I can't help but think how different their life together is from mine. They've built a beautiful family, have a warm home, and have created stability. I've always had my work, my plans, and Felix by my side, but there's something about the way they move through life with the ease of shared love and understanding that makes me wonder if I might one day have that kind of romance myself. I want a wife to share my days with and children to raise and watch grow. Perhaps someday I'll find that, too.

5

DREAMING

I open my eyes, look up at the night sky, and see two women I don't recognize leaning over me. Sharp, intense pain spikes at my temple, and I lie still for a moment, trying to piece together where the hell I am. The last thing I remember is falling into a pit at the archaeology site in the middle of the day. Nothing about this place matches that memory, and for a few seconds, I just lie here, breathing slowly as I try to make sense of it.

"Are you well, Domina?" one of the women asks. I recognize the language as Oscan, which shouldn't be possible.

"Sit her up," the other woman says.

They pull me upright, and I look around to see that we're in a narrow alley. A high wall of stone and plaster stands beside us, similar in construction to the partial wall I was working on earlier, enclosing what must be the rear of a domus.

The surfaces of the walls are fresh and clean. There's no dust, dirt, or ash covering them. They aren't broken, jagged, or buried. They look lived in, yet nearly new.

The women are dressed in clothing that looks exactly like what I've only ever seen in reenactments or movies—fabric wrapped and draped in that unmistakable style that historians and archaeologists study and actors try to recreate.

For a moment, I refuse to accept it, searching for an explanation that makes sense. Is this a staged reenactment, a demonstration, something I've stepped into without realizing it? I sit here, caught between what I know and what I'm seeing, not sure which one I'm supposed to trust.

"Where are you from, Domina?" the second woman asks.

I still can't think clearly enough to answer, and I'm afraid of what might come out if I open my mouth. I've studied the language, but I've never actually had the opportunity to speak it in conversation.

"Perhaps she struck her head," the woman says, cupping my face and tilting it gently as she examines me. "Her hair is like a cloud. White and shining."

"Yes, look at her sapphire eyes. Her clothing is odd. Perhaps she's a goddess or a guardian spirit," the other woman replies. "Shall we help her up?"

They pull me to my feet, keeping hold of my arms as they guide me out of the alley and into a winding street. The buildings are sturdy, not ruined or crumbling like I remember. The walls stand solid and freshly kept, their surfaces rough with plaster and stone, worn only by the materials they're made of, and maybe weather, but not by disaster.

Finally, we reach a narrow building set close against the others and step inside. They lead me through a tight entry that opens into a small central space, the air heavy with oil and perfume, then past a row of cramped rooms divided by thin walls before we step through a doorway. One of the women studies me for a moment,

"Why are you dressed like that?" she asks.

I stare at her. "Why are *you* dressed like that?" The words come out before I can stop them.

The women glance at each other, smirking, and then laugh, the sound light and teasing, as if they can't believe the first words out of my mouth are a jab.

I look down at my clothes–khaki pants, a worn field shirt, sturdy boots–and the laughter hits me differently. I really am the one out of place here.

"I'm Flavia, and this is Sabina," the one with her dark hair pulled back into a simple braid says. Her skin is bronzed from the sun, her tunic tied at the waist with a narrow belt. She lifts a folded stola from a wooden chest and hands it to me. "Here, you can borrow some of Tullia's clothes. You look about the same size."

"Tullia's our roommate," Sabina says, her curly dark hair tied back with a simple cord. Her skin is sun-kissed, and her stola is loose at the shoulders. "She's out working right now. She'll be home soon. What's your name?"

"My name is Fiona." I look around and realize I must be dreaming —or in a coma. This isn't a reenactment; the city still stands. This is real. I'm here, holding clothes from the Roman Imperial period.

"Here," Flavia says, gesturing toward a wooden divider at the back of the room. "You can step behind there and change."

I nod, slipping past the screen and pulling off my modern clothes. The stola feels strange in my hands, soft but heavy, and I manage to wriggle into it, adjusting the folds as best I can. When I step back out, the women are smirking, clearly entertained by how out of place I must appear.

"So, are you going to tell us where you're from?" Flavia asks, handing me a pair of sandals.

I have no idea what to say. How could I possibly tell them I'm from a place that won't exist for another two thousand years?

"I… I'm from far to the north," I finally say, slipping into the sandals, which are surprisingly only just a little too snug. "A place you probably haven't heard of."

The women glance at each other, clearly noticing how different I look.

"Is that why your hair grows white?" Sabina asks.

"Well, we call it platinum blonde where I come from," I reply, "but yes."

"It's gorgeous," Flavia adds.

"Thank you," I say. "Did you say your roommate was working?

What kind of work does a woman do at night?" I catch myself the instant the words slip out, cheeks heating, realizing how rude that must sound.

Flavia smiles. "We're courtesans."

Sabina pours something from a small clay jug into a cup and holds it out. "Would you like to have some wine with us?"

"Yes, thank you," I say, taking the cup from her hands.

I notice how they carry themselves. They're confident, unashamed, completely at ease in who they are, even in a world where women have so few choices. They have their own room here, they're beautiful and seem healthy, and they make their own way. It's clear to me that they take care of themselves, and they do it well.

I take a sip of the wine, and it's incredible. "I've never had wine that tastes so wonderful," I tell them.

"Do they not have wine like this in the north?" Sabina asks.

"Definitely not." I smile, savoring the rich, tangy sweetness that's completely unlike anything I've ever tasted.

Sabina tilts her head, studying me a little more closely. "How did you end up in that alley, anyway? And your head—does it still hurt?"

The question makes my grip tighten around the cup. I keep my expression as calm as possible. "I don't know," I lie. "I just remember waking up and seeing both of you standing over me."

Sabina's expression softens, and she nods. "Well, you're safe now."

The door opens, and another beautiful woman steps inside. Her dark hair is twisted up and piled atop her head. She wears a deep red tunic, belted at the waist, with a pale cream shawl draped over one shoulder.

"Fiona, this is Tullia," Flavia says, gesturing toward me. "Tullia, this is our guest, Fiona from the north."

Tullia smiles. "Welcome, Fiona. You've come at a good time."

Sabina tilts her head, curious. "Why is it a good time?"

Tullia grins and pulls a small pouch from her belt. "Because I just got a very handsome tip from a client," she says, holding out a bit of what looks to me like a small, dark lump in a cloth, sticky and fragrant in a strange, earthy way.

Flavia and Sabina clap their hands together, giddy, their laughter filling the room.

"Poppy sap? Well done!" Flavia cheers.

"We've earned this!" Sabina adds.

I find myself smiling, too. Their enthusiasm and energy is infectious. Then I rack my brain, trying to figure out what "poppy sap" could mean, and it suddenly hits me—these ladies are about to nibble on some opium.

Flavia grabs a wine bottle from the table in the corner of the room. "Let's take this up to the roof," she says, her eyes sparkling.

Tullia and Sabina nod and gather cushions and small blankets. The three women lead the way up a narrow staircase, and I follow, careful not to stumble, my mind spinning. The thought of walking across a rooftop in Pompeii at night, while the city is alive and whole, long before the eruption, feels completely surreal.

On the roof, I stare out across the city, dark, quiet, and still, the streets winding between the stone and plaster buildings. The women arrange the cushions in a small circle on the flat roof.

We sit, and Flavia lifts the wine bottle, taking a sip, before handing it to Tullia, who drinks before passing it to Sabina. I take my turn, tilting the bottle and tasting the sweet wine. The buzz hits me fast, and I feel it already starting to go to my head.

"So, Tullia," Sabina asks, leaning back on her elbows, "who gave you the poppy sap?"

Tullia grins. "A very generous client," she says. "A wealthy man living in a fine house not far from here." She reaches into the folds of her tunic and pulls out the sap.

When she unwraps the dark lump and bites off a portion, I watch her, wondering if I'm actually about to take a bite myself or if I'm dreaming. Maybe if I take a bite, I'll wake up, and I'll no longer be on a rooftop in ancient Pompeii with three beautiful harlots.

Flavia takes a piece next, chewing as she passes the remainder to Sabina, and I catch myself thinking that I need to quickly decide if I'm going to try opium for the first time with strangers in a strange land. Sabina nibbles hers and then holds the last piece out to me, and I realize I'm caught somewhere between curiosity and completely losing my mind.

I take a deep breath, telling myself that if I eat it, I'll wake up from whatever dream or nightmare I've fallen into. I bite off a tiny piece, chew, and immediately, a cozy warmth spreads through my head, softening the edges of the stress.

Tullia lies back, head on her cushion, eyes half-closed. "Ah, that's perfect," she murmurs, her words coming out soft and dreamy.

Flavia giggles and looks at me. "You feel it too, don't you? Light... floating..."

I try to focus on the language, but my thoughts are wild, like feathers drifting, and it takes me a moment to translate my thoughts from English to Oscan. "I... I think I see what you mean," I whisper, the words coming out slowly, as I let my body sink into the cushions. The pain in my head has completely disappeared, and I've never felt so weightless and carefree.

Sabina sighs, looking up toward the stars. "It's like the world's spinning in the palm of my hand."

One by one they stretch out on the cushions, relaxing into the warmth, eyes closing, breathing slowly. I feel my eyelids growing heavy, my thoughts softening and drifting, and I tell myself that when I wake up, I'll be back in 2026, at the dig site, with my colleagues, in the world I know.

THE SUN'S FIRST LIGHT FALLING ACROSS MY EYELIDS MUST WAKE ME because when I open them, the sky is no longer black and twinkling silver. It's orange, coral, and fuchsia. The beauty of the morning crashes into the hideousness of the terror in my heart when I realize that I'm still here with the three ladies I met last night.

How am I going to get back home?

I rise and walk to the edge of the roof, taking it all in. The city is waking, carts being loaded, shutters opening on the houses below. People move with purpose, unaware of me above them, and for a moment, I can't even be upset that I'm stuck here. It feels like a dream I don't want to leave yet, and I wonder if I'll wake up at any second.

I hear movement behind me and turn around to see Tullia stretching and yawning and Flavia standing up to smooth her tunic.

"Good morning," Tullia says, looking up at me. "Did you sleep well?"

"I think so," I reply, still dizzy from last night's wine and sap.

Sabina wakes up next, stretching and standing up to brush the dust from her clothes. She doesn't speak, and her brow is furrowed, making me think she must not be a morning person.

Tullia stands, too. "Let's go downstairs and get ready for our day."

They move toward the steps leading down from the roof, and I follow. Back in their room, they begin their morning routine.

We each dip our hands into the basins of water and splash our faces. Sabina hands me a chew stick, and I follow her example, scraping gently at my teeth as she does hers. Flavia twists her hair into a braid, securing it with pins.

Tullia pulls out a small bronze mirror and holds it up to me. "May I?" she asks, holding a pinch of reddish powder between her fingers. When I nod, she gently dabs it onto my cheeks.

After Tullia finishes with the powder, Sabina leans over and asks, "May I do your hair?

"Of course," I say, and she begins twisting sections into a braid, securing them with pins as she works.

Sabina's fingers move carefully through my hair. "Are you sure your head is all right? From when we found you?"

"It's fine," I say. "It doesn't hurt anymore."

"Do you remember anything at all?" Flavia asks. "Where you live? Your family? Your friends? Where you were coming from or going to?"

"No," I lie again, shaking my head. "I don't remember any of that. Just my name." I hesitate, then add quietly, "I'm so sorry."

Tullia waves a hand dismissively. "There's nothing to apologize for."

"Yes," Sabina agrees gently. "It's not your fault."

Flavia nods. "What matters is that you're all right. You're sure your head doesn't hurt?"

I shake my head again. "No, it's fine. I just... don't remember anything."

Sabina's tone softens. "Then we'll just have to make sure you're taken care of until you do."

When Sabina finishes with my hair, I lift the bronze mirror and stare at my reflection. I hardly recognize myself. I look like one of them, apart from the color of my eyes and hair. A thrill runs through me. This is starting to feel like an adventure, and I can't help but smile at the thought. What is a day in the life of a woman in Pompeii like? I suppose I'm about to find out.

6

ALLURING

MARCUS

Just as the sun is rising, I fall into step beside Quintus, following the priest of Venus, Spurius Atilius, through the waking streets. The early sun strikes the plaster walls, brightening the city in shades of gold and ocher. Women pass with baskets of bread and vegetables, laborers call greetings to each other, and carts creak along the stone street.

"Have you prepared the first offering?" the priest asks, glancing at me. His voice carries easily over the chaos.

"I've arranged the altars," I say. "They are near the temple steps, and the smaller one are by the fountain. It should be enough."

Quintus looks at the priest. "And the timing? When do you want the first libation poured?"

Spurius Atilius lifts a hand. "Just as the sun reaches the temple entrance. The light must touch the statue as we begin. That is the ritual's heartbeat."

A wine merchant walks over to us, rubbing the back of his neck. "The new wine is excellent. But the festival will bring crowds," he says. "I need my amphorae in a different place while the parade passes, or the barrels will be tipped over by the throng."

"We'll place your barrels on the forum's edge," I reply. "That way there's enough room for everyone. You'll need to get your barrels set up before the first libation."

He grunts, apparently satisfied. "And the offerings?"

"The first grapes go to Venus," Spurius says. "Then figs, bread, and wine in turn. Each consecration follows the other with no interruptions. The people will notice if anything is misaligned, and the gods will not be pleased."

I watch the crowd as he speaks. The merchant nods and returns to his barrels. Children chase each other in the center of the square, and a stray goat nudges its way through the crowd toward us. I weave carefully around him, keeping up with Quintus and the priest. My mind ticks through the streets, noting where congestion will build during the festival.

My friend leans close. "Marcus, you've counted the altars and the attendants?"

"I have," I answer. "Everyone is aware of their duties."

The priest chuckles softly. "You're always thinking ahead. I trust your expertise will keep the festival flowing."

"I hope so," I say. "Disorder spreads faster than a rain-swollen river."

When we walk past the animal stalls, I notice a pile of straw too close to a brazier. The festival crowds will only make it worse once the torches are lit. I step forward, nudging the straw back a few feet and warning the shepherds. "Keep the straw piles away from the fire!" I shout, pointing to the brazier.

With the morning in full swing now, the market is stirring. Merchants lift baskets of cheese, jars of honey, and bundles of herbs onto their stalls. One spreads colorful bolts of cloth. Another arranges clay lamps and small bronze utensils. A woman sweeps the steps of her taberna, while a boy carries a basket of sandals past a stand of perfumes and oils. People move with purpose, setting out their wares and waving to one another. The city is waking, each person absorbed in their tasks, and I take it all in, noting where the crowds will gather once the festival begins.

Ahead, I notice a small group of women. It's not the way they're dressed or how they speak that catches my eye, but the beauty of one of them. Her braid is long and pale, catching the sunlight like golden flower petals. It isn't dyed or powdered–it's natural, and impossibly bright. I find myself watching her a moment longer than I should.

When she turns, and I see her eyes, my jaw falls open. They are a vivid blue. I find her to be striking, though I do my best to look away. Still, every step she takes holds my gaze.

Quintus nudges me with his elbow. "Marcus, you do realize the city is full of people, yes?" he says, smirking. "Or are you studying one in particular?"

I toss him a sideways glance. "I'm... observing the people," I mutter, trying to sound authoritative.

"The market? Or the woman with the golden hair?" he teases, but I can't help but watch the woman as she follows her friends, laughing and chatting while they buy their breakfast.

Spurius stops, his eyes moving back to the temple. "I have something I need to take care of. Will you excuse me?"

"Of course," Quintus says.

"We'll handle things from here," I add.

The priest nods and slips through the crowd, disappearing from view. As he walks away, my attention drifts back to the gorgeous woman.

She's intriguing, alluring, and I can't take my eyes off her curves, the smoothness of her skin, and the way her hair, her eyes, even her lips are unlike anyone else's. I've never seen anyone like her, and I want to know everything about her.

Quintus notices I'm distracted again. "Shall we go speak with her?" he asks.

I feel my face heat. "Of course not. We have work to do."

He chuckles and shakes his head, but doesn't press the issue further. We spend the morning moving through the forum and toward the temple courtyard, checking platforms, ropes, and the placement of ceremonial vessels, making adjustments as we go. Quintus points out where attendants will need room to move on the steps, and I note which of them should handle each task when they arrive.

By midday, the courtyard feels organized, every step of the procession accounted for and no detail overlooked. We pause to rest in the shade of the temple portico, sipping water and scanning the space one last time.

The afternoon passes quickly as we walk the paths again, confirming timing and events, and ensuring everything is marked for future setup. As the sun moves westward, I step back and let myself relax, the weight of planning it all lifting from my shoulders.

"That should hold until tomorrow." I brush my hands together to remove the day's dust.

Quintus looks at me, grinning. "Are you finally dismissing me, then?"

I grin. "For the day. Go rest and say hello to your wife and children for me."

He nods, slinging his satchel over his shoulder. "I will. See you tomorrow, then."

"See you," I say with a wave.

I watch him walk off across the courtyard and then lean against the temple wall. Our work is finished. Yet, my thoughts returns to the radiant woman from this morning, and I find myself wondering about her name, where she's from, and where she might be now.

I push the thoughts of her aside and walk across the courtyard and into the street, until I see the thermopolium ahead, its awning casting shade over the entrance. I slow as I reach it and step inside. The smell of warm bread, stewed lentils, wine, and smoke hits me immediately. A few people are already gathered at tables, eating their early evening meal.

"Marcus?"

I turn at the sound of my name and find my brother, Lucius, already here, seated on a stool, cup in hand. He lifts it in greeting as I cross the room.

"Have you been here long?" I ask, taking the empty stool across from him.

"Long enough to finish one drink and begin another," he replies, setting his cup down. "You look like you've come straight from work."

"I have."

"Then you've earned this." He gestures to the counter. "Wine?"

I step up to the counter and order my dinner. The server nods as she listens, already turning to prepare it.

"I'll bring it to you when it's ready," she says.

"Thank you." I return to the table and take my seat next to my brother.

"You've been scarce lately," he says. "Is the festival planning taking up all your time and energy?"

"It's quite a bit of work," I remind him. "Let's just say I'll be relieved when it's over."

The server brings a tray and sets a bowl and bread before me. "For a man who carries the festival on his shoulders, you seem to manage well," she says, her tone light, her eyes meeting mine briefly before she bats her lashes and looks away again.

"Oh? In what way?" I ask, curious.

She smiles. "Just that you look well." I notice her cheeks turning slightly pink.

"Thank you, Domina," I reply, trying to maintain my composure.

She nods and steps away from the table, going back to her work. Lucius waits until she is out of hearing range before leaning in and lowering his voice with a grin. "Careful, Marcus. You may find yourself with admirers you didn't intend to collect."

"I think you read too much into a simple comment," I say.

"She was clearly flirting with you," my brother presses, unable to hide his amusement. "And don't you want to find a wife one day?"

"I do," I admit. "It's something I've been considering more often lately." I look at him. "What about you, Lucius? Do you see yourself marrying?"

"Me?" He leans back, startled. "I'm only twenty. I'm not some old man like you. I've hardly thought about it."

I let out a short laugh. "I'm not old. I'm twenty-seven."

"Yes, but you have a fine position, a fancy house—hell, even your dog carries himself with more dignity than most men. You're already set. A wife and children are the natural next step."

"I suppose you're not wrong," I say before taking a sip of my wine.

I look back toward the counter. The server catches my eye again, offering me a smile and a little wave. I nod to her in return.

Lucius follows my gaze and chuckles. "Perhaps Mother will get those grandchildren she's been hoping for sooner than we think." I kick him under the table, and he laughs even harder.

Fortunately for me, the rest of the meal is shared in simple conversation–talk of the festival, the small household troubles my mother has been dealing with, and Lucius's ongoing money problems.

By the time we start to run out of topics to speak about, our bowls are empty, and the last of the wine has been shared between us. Lucius pushes his bowl forward. "That should carry me through the evening," he says, rising from his stool.

I set my cup aside and stand with him. "Yes, that was a good meal."

I leave some coins on the table, and we head for the door, stepping outside and pausing just beyond the entrance.

"Goodnight, Marcus," Lucius says.

"Goodnight, Lucius," I reply. "Send Mother and Father my love."

He nods and turns to head home. I go the other way toward my house.

As I walk, my mind wanders back to the fair-haired maiden from the market this morning. I wonder why I can't stop thinking about her. Who is she, and what is this power she has over my thoughts?

7

———

FORTUNA

FIONA

I follow Flavia, Sabina, and Tullia through the market on my second morning in Pompeii, staying close as they move between the stalls, their voices overlapping as they talk to one another. Yesterday felt just as disorienting. We spent the morning here in the market, passed the afternoon in the small apartment while we did chores and talked, and then I spent an uneasy stretch of hours alone after they left for their evening work, not knowing what to do with myself or how to exist in a place where I don't belong.

"Let's get some figs first," Flavia says as she slows at a stall.

"You say that every morning," Sabina replies, glancing at the selection.

"Well, everyone knows figs are the best fruit," Flavia explains. We approach a stall, and she asks, "How much for these?"

He weighs the figs. "Three dupondii."

Flavia doesn't hesitate. "Two."

He shakes his head once. "Three."

Flavia exhales and then gives a small nod. "Fine. Three."

The vendor scoops a portion of figs into a small container and hands it over to her, accepting the coins in return.

"We'll need bread as well," Tullia says as we rejoin the flow of the crowd.

Sabina nods. "Yes. Let's go to the bakery before the better loaves are gone."

Tullia leads us, and we move away from the stalls toward a nearby shopfront where the scent of fresh bread drifts into the air. Inside, the bakery is warm, and the counter is lined with loaves of different colors, shapes, and sizes.

Tullia steps up to the counter. "I'd like a round loaf of bread, please."

The man behind the counter selects one for her and sets it down. "This one is fresh from this morning."

Tullia digs a coin out of her pouch. "It looks perfect. Thank you."

She hands him the money, and he gives her the bread. She puts it in her basket, and we turn back toward the street and the stalls beyond.

Once we're back outside in the forum, Flavia adjusts her grip on her basket and looks over at me. "Come on, Fiona. We're only just getting started."

Tullia glances down as we walk. "I need new sandals. The straps on these are giving out."

Flavia nods. "We'll go to the sandal stalls next."

Sabina adds, "There's one along the outer row. This way."

We head toward the edge of the market, where the stalls thin and rows of sandals are laid out for sale.

I follow them, but the same thought keeps invading my mind. I shouldn't be here, not in this era, not before the volcano has even erupted. The question sits there with everything else I don't know how to handle yet—what is the year, and how do I ask without raising questions I can't afford?

The question leads into the next one before I can stop my anxiety from running away. Even if I figure out what year it is, that doesn't fix anything. I don't have any money. I'm staying with ladies of the night, and they'll expect me to start doing the same work they do or come up with some other way to pay my share. People here don't just exist without work, without connections, or without some kind of role.

I don't have anyone or anything that belongs to me in this time.

I keep my expression pleasantly neutral as I walk, but my thoughts won't stay still. How do I explain who I am without sounding like a lunatic? Without raising suspicion?

The part I keep trying to push away won't stay quiet. I'm stuck here with no clear way back, no map for how to undo this or reverse whatever brought me here. Nothing I've studied tells me how to return, and nothing around me offers an answer. All I have is the fact that I'm here now, and the growing certainty that if there *is* a way home, I'm going to have to find it myself—without knowing where to start.

The thought doesn't disappear, but it recedes just enough for me to notice we've reached the next stall. Tullia steps forward, already addressing the vendor as she lifts a pair of sandals. They're soft pale leather with thin straps decorated with small gold beads and tiny colored stones that shimmer as she turns them, the ornaments glinting along the lines that cross over the foot and curve up around the ankle.

"How much for these?" she asks.

The man answers quickly, naming a price, and she doesn't hesitate before responding.

"That's too high," she purrs, leaning in. I can't tell if she's pouting or being seductive, but either way, it seems to be working. The sandals are gorgeous, so I can't say I blame her.

The vendor offers a lower amount, and Tullia nods, selects a few coins from her pouch and says, "That will do."

Sabina leans toward me and whispers, "I would've paid the first price. Those are beautiful."

I laugh under my breath at her bluntness. "Yes, they definitely are."

Tullia slips on her new sandals. "Fiona, could you please carry these? I don't want to get the bread dusty."

"I'd be happy to," I say.

She tosses her old ones in my empty basket.

Flavia shifts her basket on her shoulder, looking toward the next stall. "Come on," she says. "We're not finished yet."

We start walking again, Sabina still close beside me. "Cassius said he'd return tonight," she says, rolling her eyes.

"I think he might have eyes for you," Tullia replies, looking back at her.

"And Cassius is a wealthy man," Flavia adds.

"Most of them are, or they wouldn't be able to afford us," Sabina says, tossing her hair over her shoulder.

"Too true." Tullia laughs.

I keep my eyes forward as I listen, saying nothing, but the longer the morning goes on, the more aware I become of how little I've contributed to any of the conversation. They've been talking easily between themselves, and I've done nothing but follow along in near silence, which has to seem strange by now. I should say something—anything—but what could I possibly be contributing to this conversation? And worse—when are they going to ask me about myself and what I've been doing with my life? What will I say if they do? How long will they believe that I just don't remember anything?

I woke up this morning in their room, expecting something else entirely—either a hospital bed in my own time or the bottom of the pit I fell into—anything that would explain this as a mistake that hadn't really happened. I expected the illusion to break the moment I opened my eyes. Instead, the room remained unchanged, with the others already awake, the day already moving forward without me.

Now, as we continue through the market, I glance briefly upward toward the distant outline of Mt. Vesuvius rising above the city, still and quiet against the sky—for now.

I don't know how soon the eruption will come, and as I look at my new friends, I can't help but hope it's still far off. I follow them, staying close, trying to keep up, while the reality that I'm stuck here sinks in deeper with every step.

After we've stopped for fresh herbs, grapes, and a new bottle of wine, Flavia slows after the last row of stalls. "That's enough," she says. "We've got what we need, don't we?"

Sabina exhales. "I think we have more than enough, and it's getting too crowded."

Tullia glances over at me as we turn away. "Fiona, do you need anything before we go?"

The question catches me off guard. I shake my head quickly. "No, I'm all right, thank you."

Flavia studies me for a second and then nods. "If you think of something later, we'll come back tomorrow."

I nod, and we leave the market behind, the streets narrowing as we walk. Their conversation drifts back to tonight—who might come by, who's worth the time, as well as who isn't. Dread gnaws at my gut. They left me behind last night, but that doesn't mean they will again.

At some point, they're going to expect me to go with them, to do what they do, and I have no idea how to face that. I don't know how to refuse without making myself a burden they won't want to keep.

When we reach their room, Flavia pushes the door open, and we step inside, everyone setting their baskets down. I take in each of these stunning creatures, these beautiful, generous women, and feel even worse about what I'm about to do. I have to lie to them again.

Flavia glances toward the water jugs. "We need to get water for dinner. Who wants to come with me?"

"I'll go," I say, hoping to keep busy and helpful.

Sabina raises an eyebrow. "You sure? It's a long walk to the well."

"I'd love to help," I insist.

Tullia laughs. "It won't kill you. Besides, the water tastes better when you bring it yourself."

Flavia hands me a jug, and I follow her out into the street. The fountain is small, just a stone basin set into the wall, with water running from a short spout. Flavia fills her jug first. When it's full, I lift mine and fill it the same way. Once we both have full jugs, we start back toward their room, carrying them carefully.

When we return, we set our heavy water jugs down, and I see that Sabina has already laid out the figs, the bread, and some cheese she sliced. "This should be enough for breakfast," she says, sliding a knife back into its sheath.

Flavia moves near the fire. "I'll make some posca." She lifts a small clay pot and sets it over the flame. I watch, unsure what to do, and simply follow the others as they pick up pieces of bread and figs and sit down around the table.

The cheese is salty, the figs sweet, and the faint warmth from Flavia's pot, which is some sort of herbs mixed with vinegar that I've heard of but never tasted, drifts toward me. We eat quietly for a few minutes, the room filled with the occasional remark about the food, and I try to focus on the taste, but my blood pressure rises as the thought of tonight caves in on me.

Finally, I can't hold back. "What… what is today's date?"

"August sixteenth," Flavia says.

"That's right." I nod. "And… the year?"

She looks at me like I've lost my mind but says, "Seventy-nine–of course."

"Of course." I do the quick math in my head and drop the fig I'm holding on the floor. The city has no more than eight days left.

"Fiona, you're even paler than usual," Sabina says, her eyes filled with concern. "Are you all right?"

The words tumble out before I can stop them. "I need to tell you who I am and where I'm from now. I didn't forget before—it simply wasn't the right moment to share with you. I'm not from this time. I came from the faraway future. I know things I shouldn't. I know things that haven't happened yet."

Tullia stops chewing and leans toward me. "What are you saying, Fiona?"

"I—I was moved through time," I reply. "By Fortuna, the goddess of chance. She placed me outside of my proper hour."

I use Fortuna's name because she is the one symbol or deity I know they might believe, my one shot at being seen as touched by fate.

The three of them exchange glances, and I hold my breath.

Finally, Flavia nods. "I told you she was a guardian spirit. I said that right when we first saw her."

Sabina stares at me, her eyes filled with awe and curiosity. Then she looks back at Flavia, who is nonchalantly pouring the drinks as if I've just told them I've come from Rome rather than the future. "You did say that, Flavia. I'll give you that," Sabina says. She turns back to me. "Will you tell us of your era?"

"Now, wait a damn minute," Tullia says, setting her breakfast down and standing to step closer, examining me. She crouches to bring her face level with mine, her gaze fixed and unblinking. "How do we know you're telling the truth?"

I swallow hard and take a deep breath. "There's no way you could possibly know for certain whether anyone is telling the truth about anything," I say. "But I can promise you this—in just over a week, your city will be destroyed. And if I am still here, I will make sure your lives are spared."

Tullia straightens slowly, studying me for a moment, then she nods. "You are right," she says, her tone softer now. "One can never fully know whether someone speaks honestly or not."

"Well, I believe you, Fiona," Sabina says.

"As do I," Flavia adds. "What reason would she have to lie to us, Tullia? She can't be a criminal. We have nothing to steal."

"Oh, all right," Tullia says. "You won't hear me call you a liar, Fiona."

Relief crashes through me, but it's fragile. "Thank you," I say.

Sabina looks worried now. "Then tell us—what did you mean? You said our city will be destroyed. By which of the gods?"

Tullia looks me in the eye. "Yes. If you expect us to believe you, you will explain."

I hesitate, but then force the words out. "There's a mountain… just outside the city."

"All of Italia has mountains," Tullia snaps. "What about it?"

"It's not just a mountain," I say. "It's a volcano, and it's going to erupt."

Sabina looks confused. "Erupt?"

"It will explode," I say. "There will be fire, ash, smoke—everything will be thrown into the sky. The ash will fall back down over the city and bury everyone and everything."

Flavia's face turns pale. "Everyone?"

"Yes. The ground will shake. The sky will turn black. You won't be able to breathe."

"That's—" Sabina shakes her head, backing up a step. "That's not real. That can't be real."

Tullia stares at me, her confidence slipping. "What is this mountain called?"

"Vesuvius."

Flavia grips Sabina's arm. "If this is true—if even part of it is true—"

"The gods would warn us," Sabina says quickly.

"Maybe they are," Flavia whispers.

"Then we're going to the temple. First thing in the morning," Tullia says.

Sabina nods. "Yes. The priest of Venus will know what to do."

"You will come with us. You will tell him everything," Tullia adds.

"I will," I say.

I feel terrible for lying to them about Fortuna. They seem like such amazing women, but I want to be able to protect them—and myself—when the time comes.

The morning had started with the fear that I might have to sell myself just to make it through the night. But now, as I sit here, that seems laughable. What does it matter? In just over a week, the city will be nothing but ash and rubble. I'm not going to survive this. None of us is. And here I am, caught in a time I don't belong in, with no way out, and no clue how to stop the volcano that's about to end Pompeii.

8

OPPORTUNITY

Marcus

I walk down the street toward my parents' house with my dog Felix at my side, just as the sun rises over Pompeii. People are waking, and a rooster crows somewhere nearby. I haven't seen my parents in a few days because of work, and I promised I'd join them for breakfast this morning. The house comes into view, its shutters open, servants already moving about in the garden.

As we reach the door, Felix must already smell the breakfast cooking inside—he stops with his nose in the air, sniffing. I push the door open, step inside, and am immediately met by the smell of fried eggs and freshly baked bread.

When I walk into the dining room, my parents are already seated at the table. "Marcus, come join us," my mother calls.

"Sit. We were just about to start," my father adds.

I walk over and take my seat at the table. "Where is Lucius?" I ask.

My mother shakes her head as Lydia sets her breakfast plate in front of her. "Your brother came home late last night again. He's still asleep." She glances at the servant. "Thank you, Lydia."

The girl nods and serves Father and me breakfast. We both thank her, and she bows and leaves the room.

"How late did Lucius get home?" I ask.

"Past midnight," my father says, frowning. "He keeps coming home at all hours. We believe he's gambling again. We're worried about him."

My mother's face drops. "Last week, he came home with a black eye. We can't have this continuing."

I rub my hand down the back of my neck, feeling a flash of concern. "I'll talk to him. I'll make him understand."

"You must, Marcus," my father says. "He gives the wrong men a reason to rough him up, and he doesn't see the danger he's bringing the whole family. You're his older brother. He listens to you."

"I will," I say. "I'll make him listen."

My mother softens slightly. "Thank you, Marcus. Just… warn him carefully. He won't listen if you lecture. But make him see the consequences."

I smile at her. "Don't worry, Mother. I'll handle it."

After we've spoken about Lucius, the conversation shifts to lighter topics. We chat about the garden, the olives and grapes this year, and the upcoming festival. I comment on the plans for the city's preparations, and my parents nod, asking questions about what's already arranged and what still needs attention. The morning passes quickly, the conversation flowing naturally while we finish our meal and prepare to move on with the day.

We are almost finished with breakfast when my mother smiles and says, "Thank you for coming, Marcus. We know how busy you are."

"Yes, my son," Father adds. "We certainly do love it when you stop by and share a meal with us."

"Of course," I reply. "After the festival, I'll have more time to spend with you and Lucius."

I feed the last piece of my egg to Felix under the table. He swallows it down eagerly with a little yelp of gratitude. "I need to head to the temple," I say. "Work won't wait."

My father nods. "Go, but remember your promise. Lucius needs you."

"Yes, Father." I stand and head for the door. Felix follows me, and we step out into the sunlight. The day stretches before me, bright, and full of opportunity.

My dog and I walk through the city, passing the forum on our way to the temple. When we arrive, I stop at the bottom of the steps. "Stay here," I tell him, and he sits, watching me without moving. I climb the steps, where Quintus is already waiting at the top.

"Good morning, Marcus," he says when I reach him. "Ready to see the priest?"

"Yes. We need to finalize the sequence of events for the festival— offerings, dances, priestly duties. Everything must be precise."

Quintus nods. "The attendants and musicians are all ready. The priest just needs to confirm the order."

We step inside the temple together. The priest of Venus, Spurius Atilius, stands near the altar. He inclines his head in greeting as we approach. "Marcus, Quintus. Good morning. Is everything prepared for the festival?"

"All set," I say. "But I want to review the opening rites. The offerings, the sacrifices, the order of events."

Atilius nods. "Understood. Which do you wish to begin with?"

"The offerings first. I want the priestesses in position and the attendants ready before any procession starts."

"When they arrive," Quintus says, "we'll place them under your direction."

Atilius steps closer to the altar, motioning to the ceremonial spaces. "Follow me, Marcus. We'll go through it step by step."

I move with him, checking positions. Quintus writes notes, walking beside me, and we go through the order of every ritual, every prayer, and every song.

Satisfied, I'm ready to move on with the rest of my workday. "Everything seems in order."

Spurius Atilius nods. "Excellent. The festival will proceed smoothly under your guidance, Marcus."

"Thank you, Spurius. We'll be ready."

Quintus and I walk toward the temple doors, and as we step back outside, the sunlight hits my face. I blink a few times and look around for Felix, hoping he'd stayed where I told him to wait. That's when I see her—the beautiful woman from the market. Her hair is nearly white, falling down her back in soft curls, and her eyes shine blue as the sky. She's crouched down, petting Felix, surrounded by three friends.

"Training your dog to catch you a wife. Very clever, Marcus." Quintus chuckles, and I elbow him in the ribs.

We walk toward them, and one of the women looks up. "Is this your dog?"

I step closer. "Yes, his name is Felix. I hope he was behaving himself."

Another woman smiles. "Of course. He's a perfect gentleman and adorable."

"Thank you," I reply, kneeling to ruffle Felix's ears.

The first woman gestures toward the temple. "Is the priest of Venus in there? Our friend"–she motions to the stunning blonde woman who is even more elegant and alluring up close– "needs to speak with him."

"Yes," I say. "He's in the temple. You can go right in."

"Thank you." She looks at me then, the striking woman who was just petting my dog, and my breath catches in my throat.

I almost talk myself into asking her name, but before I can get the words out, the four women have disappeared into the temple.

Morning stretches into afternoon. Quintus and I are still working, seeing to the last of the festival preparations, checking what's been hung, what still needs doing, what might fall apart if left alone. Felix trails after us the whole while with his nose to the ground, as if he has some duty of his own to inspect every corner.

The sun climbs high, and the heat settles in, so we return to Quintus's house for the midday meal. Cornelia has outdone herself again, the table laid with more than we could reasonably consume, and we eat well. Little Gaius and Julia play in the backyard with Felix, and the dog bounds after them as though he understands he is part of their game.

When at last we rise from the table, the sun is starting its downward trajectory across the sky. What remains of the day passes quickly, work keeping us busy until the light begins to fade from the streets. By evening, the noise of the market softens, and Quintus and I exchange a few final words before turning off in different directions, each of us making for home as dusk settles over the city.

The forum is quiet now, the last merchants gone, their stalls shuttered and bare. I walk the familiar route home, Felix at my side. The city seems to fall asleep at this hour. Doors are closing, lamps are being lit in the windows, and voices are lower and less enthusiastic in the streets.

Felix stiffens beside me, stops in his tracks, and the hair on the back of his neck stands up. He bares his teeth, and a low growl escapes his throat. I glance around, scanning the shadows and empty streets, but I see nothing out of the ordinary. "Relax, Felix," I murmur, placing my hand on his head.

I keep walking, but something seems… off. I can't tell what it is exactly, but there's an uneasy prickle on the back of my neck that tells me there's something just not right.

I pass a side street, the corner dim and littered with scraps of wood and broken pottery. Then I hear a grunt, a loud groan, and the scrape of sandals against stone.

Felix snarls. "Stay close," I whisper, my hand brushing his fur. We move toward the sound cautiously, the alley narrowing with each step. It sounds like someone's in trouble, and I catch movement—a definite struggle.

Two men have someone pressed against the wall, one twisting his tunic, the other striking him. A third stands just behind them, his arms crossed, watching. I clench my fists, a sudden rush of anger and protective instinct I can't suppress running through me, and then I recognize him—Lucius.

I move up behind them before they even notice, slamming my hands into the shoulders of the two men holding Lucius, twisting and shoving until one crashes into the wall, and the other trips over his own feet. Felix darts at their legs, snapping at their ankles, forcing them to stagger backward.

The third man spins around, ready to strike, but seeing Felix circling and my fists raised, he hesitates. I push the first two toward the alley mouth, driving them away from Lucius.

The tallest one leers at me. "And who's this? Your older brother?"

I step closer, planting myself between Lucius and them. "Yes, I am. Back off. Now!"

The man glances at Felix, whose teeth gleam in the fading light. For a moment, I see uncertainty cross their faces. "He owes us," one of them says, trying to sound confident.

"I don't care what he owes. You touch him again, you'll deal with me," I promise. Felix lunges just enough to show the parts of him that make him more wolf than dog, and the men stumble back, fear creeping into their faces.

"Fine, fine," the leader says. He wipes his hands on his pants, scowling. "But this isn't over. Next time, your big brother won't be here, Lucius, and we'll take what's ours."

"Keep your hands off him, or you'll regret it," I spit.

The three men retreat into the shadows, their footsteps fading. I catch Lucius before he collapses, holding him up as his knees buckle. Blood drips from his mouth and nose, his eyes nearly swollen shut, and I can feel how fragile his body is—each shallow breath coming with a sharp hitch that suggests his ribs might be broken. He sways violently, almost passing out, his legs trembling uncontrollably.

"You're badly injured." I growl, gripping him tighter.

"I... I'm fine," he gasps, his voice barely audible, but his body says everything he can't.

I support Lucius under his arms as we make our way through the streets, each step slow and careful. He leans heavily against me, barely able to stay on his feet, his bloodied face and bruised eyes telling me how close he came to being killed.

Felix follows us protectively, and as we approach our parents' house, one of the servants in the garden catches sight of us. His eyes are filled with concern when he realizes how injured Lucius is, and together, we guide my brother through the doorway.

Undoubtedly drawn by the noise of our arrival, my mother and father appear in the atrium. Their faces drain of color at the sight of Lucius. Mother looks at his bloodied face. Her voice shakes as she exclaims, "Lucius! By Jupiter, what have they done to you?"

I can't answer that right now, so we carry Lucius into his room and carefully lay him down on his bed, propping him up with pillows.

My father kneels beside him, checking his limbs and ribs carefully. "Can you breathe? Where else are you hurt?"

Lucius lies there, nearly losing consciousness, blackened eyes barely open, blood trickling from his nose and mouth, each breath shallow and labored. He does not respond.

The servant fetches water and clean cloths, handing them to Mother. She weeps softly as she tries to staunch the bleeding. "He's hurt badly," she whispers, tears slipping down her cheeks.

"He'll be all right." My voice is firm as I try to comfort both my brother and our parents. "He'll heal. We'll get him through this."

Felix lays on the floor next to Lucius's bed, watching over him in case more trouble arises.

I step back, letting my parents tend to my brother, and for a moment, my thoughts drift. I think of driving those men off, of keeping Lucius safe, and all the festival preparations that demand my attention. I have so much to do, so much to keep track of. It's all quite stressful.

And then my mind wanders to that beautiful blonde woman at the temple. Who is she, and what business did she have with the priest? Overwhelmed by the day's events, and consumed by concern for my brother, my parents, and even the city itself, I slump into a bedside chair, unable to make my mind slow down.

Finally, I summon the energy to ask. "Is there anything I can do to help, Mother?"

After dabbing the last of the blood from Lucius's face, she looks at me. "You can bury the men who did this."

9

DESTINY

FIONA

This morning, Flavia, Sabina, Tullia, and I went to the temple just after first light, hoping to catch the priest of Venus before his schedule filled with preparations for the upcoming festival. From studying Pompeii, I knew that just before the eruption, the Feriae Augusti and the Vinalia Rustica took place, honoring Venus and Jupiter, so I expected the temple and the priests to be fully occupied— and we wanted to see if we could speak with him before he became too busy.

When we reached the temple, we spotted the cutest little wolf-like dog lying on the steps, and we couldn't resist crouching to pet him. While we were playing with the dog, two handsome men came out of the temple and walked toward us, and I realized he belonged to one of them. Both of the men were incredibly masculine and gorgeous, one of them particularly catching my eye. When he spoke to me, I felt the urge to stay and talk, but I shook it off as foolish and kept focused on my mission. After all, we're all going to be dead soon as it stands.

When we stepped inside the temple, we could see that it was already busy. Attendants moved in and out carrying baskets and trays as they discussed arrangements, and a handful of priestesses stood talking about the festivals.

We didn't get far before one of the priest's personal attendants intercepted us. He was polite, but firm, explaining that the priest was occupied with festival preparations today and wouldn't be available to meet. I tried to press, just a little, but he shook his head and told us we'd have better luck if we returned around sunset, when the situation had settled, and the priest might have time to speak with us properly—so we left.

We walked back to the small apartment, and the rest of the day passed as usual–with meals and chores. The women seem certain the priest of Venus can help us, or at least offer guidance, but I'm not convinced. I wonder if he will even understand what I'm asking—or if he will think I'm crazy. I wonder if he can help me find a way back to 2026 or if I'm stuck here forever.

Now, as the light is fading from the sky, we make our way back to the temple again. The streets have grown quiet, the earlier rush giving way to something calmer and slower. Flavia walks beside me, Sabina and Tullia just ahead, all of us hoping this time we can speak with the priest and gain some clarity on my situation.

We reach the temple just as the last rays of sun slip behind the rooftops. Pushing open the heavy doors, we step inside and immediately notice how much less noisy it is than this morning.

An attendant is speaking with a visitor at one of the shrines when he looks up and approaches us, his expression polite but wary. "What brings you ladies here this evening?" he asks.

"We need to speak with the priest of Venus, please," Flavia says.

The attendant nods. "I'll check to see if the priest is taking visitors." He leaves and comes back a little while later. "The priest is exhausted," he says. "He said he will see one of you, but not all four."

All three sets of eyes fall on me. Sabina says, "Fiona, you're the one who must speak with the priest."

"Yes," I agree. "I'll go," I say.

The attendant leads me past the flickering braziers and into a small chamber behind the main altar. The shadows dance across the walls, and the air is filled with incense. The priest sits behind a large desk, head bowed, shoulders slumped, his eyes half-lidded with fatigue.

He looks up as I approach and gives me a tired smile. "Come in. Please, have a seat."

I step forward and lower myself into the chair across from him.

He leans back and asks, "What is your name?"

"I am Fiona," I begin, and pause only long enough to gather myself.

"And what have you come to ask of me, child?" the priest asks.

There's nothing left to do but blurt it out. "I have come to tell you that I am from the future. I traveled more than two thousand years into the past from my time. I believe I was sent to warn everyone in the city that, within days, the mountain above Pompeii—Vesuvius— will erupt, destroying the city. Many will die if nothing is done."

He raises a brow, and I catch the faintest smirk. "From the future," he says, tone amused. "How…intriguing. Surely a young woman like you is accustomed to telling such tales?"

"I am not telling tales," I insist, urgency sharpening my words. "I'm telling the truth. You must warn the people, or they will be buried in dust and ash."

He moves his eyes over me slowly, stopping to stare at my chest, and my stomach churns. Suddenly, I realize the attendant must have told him a group of ladies of the night were waiting to speak with him, and now he thinks I'm willing.

"And what do you expect of me, girl?" he sneers. "You come here offering prophecy, and yet I should… what? Be grateful? Have faith in words like yours?" The hunger in his gaze makes my skin crawl. "Do you imagine I could give weight to words born of delirium? No doubt some potion or herb has muddled your senses," he adds, and the leer in his eyes makes my blood run cold.

I glare at him. "I'm only trying to help by telling you what I know, to warn and protect the people in this city. I may sound mad, but I'm not. Within the week, the city will fall. If you don't do anything about it, you'll be the one to blame."

He rises from his seat and circles the desk toward me, his mouth open, tongue flicking over his lips in a grotesque, predatory way. I recoil, but he's on me before I can stand, straddling my left leg with his robes draped over my lap. The priest's hand darts for my breast, but I slam it away. I spring to my feet, shouting, "I'm not yours to do with as you please! And you will regret not listening to me! Pompeii will fall!" I try to run, but he's faster than I am, and his lust is replaced by rage.

"Madness!" he hisses. "Impiety! You come here with your stories of destruction and pretend the gods care what you say. Do you know what could happen if such claims were repeated to a judge?" He leans even closer, his voice sharp as a knife. "Imprisonment. Exile. Worse! I could have you killed!"

I spin on my heel, my heart pounding, and flee the chamber. The door slams behind me, echoing through the temple. When I burst into the main sanctuary where Sabina, Tullia, and Flavia are waiting, I shout "We're leaving—now!" They follow, and we hurry out of the temple into the empty, shadowed streets.

We rush quickly back toward their room. Sabina walks beside me. "Fiona... what happened?"

I shake my head, trying not to cry. "He wouldn't believe me... and he tried to take advantage of me."

Tullia looks at me, concern in her eyes. "What? Are you hurt?"

"No, I'm not hurt. I just want to get back to your room," I say, tears brimming my eyes.

Sabina takes my hand and squeezes it. "We've all faced that at some point. It never gets any easier, but you don't have to face it alone."

I squeeze her hand back. "Thank you."

By the time we reach their room, the sun has fully set, and the stars are beginning to peek out. We step inside, and Sabina pours four glasses of wine while the rest of us find a place to sit, completely exhausted and defeated.

"What do we do now?" Tullia asks, taking her glass from Sabina.

"We could speak with a priestess of Venus or the priestess of

Jupiter. They'll be available during the festival," Sabina offers. "They might know what to do."

Flavia nods. "Or perhaps someone older and wiser. One of the elders of the city. Perhaps one of them can guide us."

Sabina hands me my wine, and I sip, trying to calm myself down. "Thank you, Sabina," I choke out.

"We could pray," Tullia says. "We could ask Fortuna why she sent you here. Maybe she'll help by giving you more instruction."

"I appreciate all your help and everything you've tried. I appreciate your friendship—and especially that you believe me," I say.

As silence falls like a veil over the room, I realize I'm trapped here —stuck in this time. Soon, they'll ask me to work the streets, and the thought makes me feel even more nauseous than when the priest tried to grope me. I glance at Sabina, Tullia, and Flavia. I care for them already, and I don't want to lose them to Mt. Vesuvius.

Finally, Flavia sets her glass down and looks around the room. "What should we have for dinner?" she asks, the question light, but practical—something we can focus on to push the heaviness aside.

Sabina leans back in her chair, stretching her arms overhead. "We've got bread, cheese, olives, and there's a little bit of fish left. That'll do. We just need to throw something together."

Tullia nods, already standing and moving toward the small kitchen area. "I'll get the fire going, and we can cook the fish. Shouldn't take long."

I rise to help, the motion automatic. There's a comfort to helping them that gives my mind a break from the constant worry. Flavia stands, too, grabbing the bread and cheese to cut while I move to the small cupboard and pull out a couple of bowls. I pour olives and figs into them, making sure there's enough for everyone. Sabina opens another bottle of wine, and the four of us work together to get a meal on the table in no time.

Once everything's ready, we sit down again, the table lit by the soft glow of a candle. Sabina's first to break the silence. "So, Fiona," she begins, "how much time do we have? How soon until it happens?"

I pause for a moment, setting my glass down before I answer. "We've got about a week. Maybe less. It'll start with tremors—the earth shaking. They'll be small at first and will go unnoticed. Then the ash will begin to fall like snow from above, and eventually everything will turn dark. The mountain will send down waves of superheated fire and ash —faster than any storm, hotter than any forge. They will sweep through the streets and into the houses. The air itself will burn so fiercely that it kills in a single breath. Anyone caught in it will die almost instantly, their bodies twisted in pain, and then the ash will bury everything so deeply that the city will vanish for centuries. There will be no time to run once those burning clouds reach us. We must leave before the mountain truly awakens—head to the north while we still can."

I watch as the three of them stare at me, their mouths hanging open.

"I'm sorry. I shouldn't have been so graphic, but I just wanted you to understand what we're up against," I add.

"No matter what happens, we're getting out of here before that mountain decides to destroy the city," Flavia says, her voice a little shaky. "We'll take our families and leave. We'll get out before it's too late."

I nod, meeting her eyes. "I'll help you however I can, but we'll need to move fast. Once the tremors start, our time is running out."

Tullia clears her throat, trying to shake off the gravity of the threat. "We'll figure it out," she says with more determination than I expect. "And we'll have each other. That's what matters, right?"

Sabina nods, forcing a smile. "Exactly. And once we're out, we'll have to make sure we have enough food, water... somewhere to stay...." She pauses, glancing over at Flavia. "It's not going to be easy, is it?"

"Perhaps we can find a nice spot on the coast. A place we can live without worrying about rocks raining down on us," Flavia says, clearly trying to see the silver lining.

I let out an appreciative sigh at her attempt to lighten the mood. "That sounds perfect," I reply.

Flavia reaches for the wine bottle, refilling our cups. "Right," she says, smiling a little more. "Well, we've got a few days, at least. Let's make sure we're ready."

The tension eases, and the topic shifts slowly from the eruption to the rest of the evening. "We're going out after dinner," Tullia says, looking at me. "You don't have to join us, Fiona. I know it's not for everyone, but if you're going to stay with us when we leave, you'll have to find some sort of work."

I glance at each of them. The thought of working the streets, of doing what they do, makes my stomach start to hurt again. "I understand. I'll figure something out."

Sabina smiles, nodding. "Good. We'll help you find something."

"I can't thank the three of you enough," I say, my relief so overwhelming, I could cry.

When the meal is over, we clear the table, collecting the empty dishes. It's strange how quickly I've come to care for and rely on these women in this foreign time.

As they prepare to leave for the night, it hits me. Maybe I was sent back just for them—to help them through this devastation. After all, they are the only ones who have listened to me, believed me, and they're the only ones helping me. Maybe destiny—or the gods—really did send me back in time just for Flavia, Sabina, and Tullia.

10

COMPLICATED

MARCUS

I wake with a stiff neck and an ache in my back, the chair unforgiving beneath me. For a moment I don't remember where I am, and then I see Lucius lying asleep in the bed, beaten and bruised, and it all comes rushing back. I remember saving my brother from being torn apart by three goons last night, and instantly, the rage returns.

Morning light blazes through the window, too bright and too soon. I drag a hand over my face and lean forward, checking on Lucius again. Tonight, the festival begins, and I have too much to do today, too many duties I can't ignore, but none of it matters as much as my brother's health and safety.

Felix is on the floor at the foot of the bed. His ears twitch as he watches Lucius. He lifts his head when I move, as if he's checking that I've got everything under control.

A soft knock at the door has me standing. I glance back at Lucius before pushing myself up and crossing the room, careful not to make more noise than necessary. When I open it, Lydia stands on the other side with a tray in her hands.

I step back to let her in, lowering my voice. "Come in."

She moves past me quietly and sets the tray down on the bedside table before turning back to me. "I have brought breakfast for your brother," she says, just as softly. "Your parents also request your presence in the dining room."

I nod once. "Thank you, Lydia."

She bows and leaves. As the door clicks shut, Lucius stirs, groaning and blinking his eyes open.

"How do you feel?" I ask, stepping closer.

He gives a faint, crooked smile. "It's not as bad as it looks. I'm fine."

My jaw tightens. "You could've *died*. There were three of them and one of you."

He's glowering at me already, and he's only just woken up. "Thank you for saving me, Marcus," he says. "But I'm fine. I'll see you at the festival tonight."

"No," I say immediately. "You need to stay home. You've got to lay low and recover."

He exhales sharply, annoyance flashing across his face. "I said I'm fine, and I'll see you at the festival tonight."

I stare at him for a long moment, frustration and worry tangling in my heart. Shaking my head, I say, "We're not finished with this conversation, but I can't stand here and argue with you right now. Some of us have work to do." I turn and walk out, the duties of the day already pressing down on me.

Felix follows me into the hall, brushing past my legs as I move. When we step into the dining room, my mother looks up from her plate and gives me a forced smile. "Good morning, Marcus."

"Good morning, Mother." I slide into the chair across from my father.

"Is Lucius awake?" she asks, concern in his eyes.

"Yes," I say. "He's awake, claiming he's fine and talking about attending the festival tonight like a complete and total fool."

"He keeps getting himself into trouble." Mother sighs and takes a sip from her glass.

"I know." I pick at the eggs Lydia has set before me. "I can't leave him to his own stupidity. He's cocky and smug about it. He thinks he can handle everything until he needs me, and then after I save him, he immediately forgets that actions have consequences. What if I'm not here next time?"

"We'll have to get through to him somehow," my father says. "He *must* learn."

I jab at my eggs, frustration churning tighter in my gut while my mind spins to the night ahead—the banners, stalls, schedules, and events. Everything has to be perfect tonight, and meanwhile, my brother puts himself in danger like a child.

"You should be careful out there, too, Marcus," my mother says. "Our whole family shares every enemy your brother has made."

"I am always careful, Mother," I mutter.

Felix rests his head on my knee, and I give him pieces of bread and eggs from my plate.

For the remainder of the meal, I silently think about the predicament my brother has landed me in this time. I shouldn't have to watch my back today with the festival starting tonight and with everything I'm supposed to manage. And now, because of Lucius, there are people looking for trouble—people I didn't have to deal with before. Every task, every detail I've planned, now comes with a shadow I didn't invite. It's infuriating.

I push my plate aside. "That's enough for me," I say. "I should get going."

"Have a good day, Marcus," my mother says softly, her eyes following me as I rise.

"I will, Mother. You as well." I manage a smile for her.

"We'll see you at the festival tonight," my father says.

"Yes," I say. "I'll see both of you at the festival tonight." Felix follows me when I move toward the door. "Goodbye for now." I glance back at my parents.

They wave, but I can see the worry in their wrinkled brows.

Outside, the morning air is warm, and the city awakens around us as we head toward the forum. By the time we reach the square, the stalls are set, performers are tuning instruments, and the vendors are arranging their goods.

Quintus is already moving among the tents, checking ropes and giving instructions to the merchants. I join him, walking past the tables lined with fresh bread and jars of honey, making sure nothing poses a hazard or is out of place.

"Good morning, Marcus," he says, glancing up as I approach.

"Good morning, Quintus," I reply. "Is everything in place?"

"For the most part."

I look over at the performers. "And the musicians? Are they all here?"

"They're giving their instruments a final tuning," he says. "They'll start soon so people will begin to drift in."

We move through the forum, making small adjustments here and there. Felix trots at my side, sniffing at the stalls with meat and bread. I keep one eye on him so that he doesn't sneak a bite and one on the crowd that's starting to gather. I don't want to be caught off guard if the thugs who roughed up Lucius last night try to jump me.

Mid-morning, a familiar voice calls out. "Quintus! Marcus!"

Cornelia approaches, basket in hand, Julia and Gaius skipping beside her. "We brought a little lunch," she says. "We thought you might need a break."

"Perfect timing," Quintus says, smiling. "We've been running around all morning."

"Thank you, Cornelia. That was very thoughtful." I kneel to greet the children. Julia tugs at my sleeve, Gaius waves enthusiastically, and Felix sniffs them. When he realizes they're not the ones holding the food, he settles at my feet.

We spread a cloth near the edge of the forum. Cornelia sets down the basket and hands Julia and Gaius figs and grapes. We eat while the crowd grows noisier around us. People are starting to gather for the evening events.

When we all have our fill, and even Felix can't eat another bite, Quintus and I stand. "Time to get back to it," I say.

Quintus hugs his children, and Cornelia tucks everything back in the basket. "I'll see you around sunset?" he asks his wife.

"Yes. We'll be here." She rises on her toes to kiss his cheek. He hugs her, and then Cornelia and the children disappear into the crowd.

Quintus and I move back into the heart of the forum, Felix close by my side. It's late afternoon, and the square continues to fill with people.

A sharp voice cuts through the racket. "I said those amphorae go there! Step back!"

Another voice responds, equally sharp, "I was here first! You can't claim more than your share!"

I glance at Quintus, and he frowns, saying, "Looks like we have our first problem of the evening."

We push through the crowd, Felix weaving between legs. Two vendors are arguing over the placement of their goods—barrels of wine and a table of olives. Their shouts rise, drawing a small gathering of early visitors.

"Enough!" I call, raising my hands. The vendors snap toward me, heat in their eyes.

Quintus steps in, his voice calm but firm. "There's room for both of you. We'll adjust the tables. Move the amphorae three feet that way. Shift your olive table to the left. That keeps the walkway clear and your customers happy."

Reluctantly, the merchants comply, grumbling, but the argument dissolves as quickly as it flared.

"We have the same problems every year," I mutter to Quintus.

"Yes," he agrees. "You'd think they'd just get along and enjoy themselves. It's supposed to be fun."

I nod and look around once more, making sure no unwanted visitors are watching me.

By the time the sun dips lower, the forum has taken on the energy of the festival. Jugglers practice tosses near the fountain, musicians are playing fast-paced tunes to draw more people, and dancers stretch their limbs at the edges of the square. The smell of sweet pastries mingles with the scent of meat roasting over the fires. Children play on the grass, and Felix chases some older boys, eager for the ball they're tossing.

I spot my parents in the crowd and walk over to them. "Everything looks wonderful," my mother says with a smile.

My father claps me on the shoulder. "You've done a fine job, Marcus."

"Thank you," I reply. "How's Lucius? Is he really planning to come tonight?"

"He's up and moving around," my father says. "We tried to stop him from coming, but he said he would come later, no matter how much we begged him not to."

"I just hope he stays home," I mutter, irritation rushing through me.

"I hope so, too," Mother says quietly, giving me a sympathetic look.

My father rubs his stomach and glances around. "I'm starving. Let's find something to eat."

"We'll see you later, Marcus," my mother adds, and Father nods, already wandering off to find dinner.

I realize I need to find Felix, whom I haven't seen in a little while. Scanning the crowd, I see a familiar face, but it's not his.

The beautiful blonde woman stands in front of the jugglers, laughing and joking with her friends. I can't help but pause for a moment, captivated. She is exquisitely, intriguingly, and ethereally beautiful. I decide not to let another chance to speak with her slip away. I take a deep breath and walk over to her.

"Hello," I say, bowing my head. "I don't believe we've formally met. I am Marcus."

She looks up at me, smiling warmly. "Hello, Marcus. I'm Fiona."

"Fiona," I repeat, letting the name roll off my tongue. "That's a beautiful name."

"Thank you," she replies.

I glance toward the grassy area where I last saw Felix. "I—uh—could use a hand finding my dog. Would you like to help?"

She tilts her head, eyes bright. "Of course. Let's see if we can track him down."

We move through the growing crowd, scanning between the festival-goers and around the edges of the square. A few minutes later, we spot Felix, crouched low and pulling enthusiastically on a rope with some children, his tail wagging furiously.

"Felix!" I call. He pricks up his ears, drops the rope, and trots over to me.

Fiona kneels down to pet him. "He's a lively one." She smiles up at me.

"He loves attention," I reply. "And he clearly likes you."

She laughs. "He must be a good judge of character. We don't have dogs like him where I'm from."

"Oh? I've seen you around, and I must admit, I was curious about where you're from," I say. "You don't look like the other women from around here."

"It's complicated. I'm from a place far away," she replies, still stroking Felix's head.

"North of here?" I ask.

She hesitates for a moment, then nods. "Yes. Far north." She stands. "Well, I should get back to my friends."

"We'll walk you back." I fall into step beside her, guiding her toward the group of women still gathered by the jugglers.

When we reach her friends, I look into her sapphire eyes. "Thank you for helping me find my dog. I hope I see you again sometime."

She smiles. "You're welcome, and I hope so, too."

"Goodbye for now, Fiona," I say.

"Goodbye, Marcus." Her smile lingers as she turns back toward the entertainers.

As Felix and I move away to find Quintus, walking through the crowd and carefully sidestepping carts and people, I can't help but feel a glimmer of satisfaction. Out of all the irritation, frustration, and exhausting demands of the day—Lucius's recklessness, the merchants' quarrels, the endless preparations for the festival—I got to speak with Fiona. I got to see her smile, learn her name, and share a few moments that weren't overshadowed by worry or duty. For a brief, shining instant, everything else fades, and the day feels worth it. No matter what happens this evening, speaking with Fiona made my night.

1 1

ENVY AND REGRET

FIONA

Marcus disappears into the crowd with his dog, Felix, trotting obediently at his side, and I feel a flutter in my chest that I try, and fail, to ignore. Flavia elbows me lightly in the ribs. "Well?" she says, her eyes sparkling with mischief. "That rich man seems quite taken with you, doesn't he?"

I flush, looking down at my hands. "I—he's just being polite."

Sabina laughs, shaking her head. "Polite? He practically tripped over himself to talk to you!"

Tullia grins, linking her arm with mine. "You're blushing, Fiona. This is new."

"I am not!" I protest, though the warmth in my cheeks says otherwise. "He's just… he's very nice, that's all."

The three of them exchange knowing looks, clearly unconvinced, but they let the topic drop, and we wander deeper into the festival. The sun is disappearing, throwing amber light across the square. Jugglers flip and toss objects, musicians play happy tunes, and the scent of several varieties of foods—everything from lamb to mulsum —wafts through the air. I let myself relax for a moment, savoring the joy all around me.

"This is incredible," Flavia says, pointing to the dancers. "I could watch this all night."

"I know," I say quietly, taking in the performance. My thoughts drift back to Marcus, though, and his gorgeous smile. I think of the way he spoke to me like I was more than just a passing stranger, and shake my head, wondering why he chose me out of all the beautiful women here. It's probably just the color of my hair, but whatever caught his attention, I'll take it.

Sabina buys a basket of candied fruit. "Come on, Fiona! You can't let us eat these without you."

I take a bite of a sugary-sweet fig. 'Thank you,' I murmur, savoring the taste.

We stroll among the stalls, and Tullia barters for a small trinket shaped like a wolf while Flavia persuades a vendor to let her sample a pastry before she buys it. I follow along, smiling. I've read every account and studied every map of this city—but walking the streets and seeing the festival alive around me is unlike anything I ever could've imagined.

After we've sampled many different types of food, listened to the band, and watched three groups of dancers, Flavia looks at me. "Fiona," she says, "we hate to leave you, but we're heading to work. The festival brings more men—more customers. You could make a few coins yourself if you go with us, you know."

I stiffen, my stomach flipping over at the mention of selling my body. "I… I'm so sorry, but I can't."

Tullia rests a hand on my shoulder. "It's all right, Fiona. We understand."

I nod, fighting back tears. My heart aches with the guilt of depending on them, the fear of having to do what they have to do to survive, and the memory of everything I've lost. "I'll try to find work elsewhere," I promise.

"We know you will. Don't worry. We'll see you soon, Fiona," Flavia says.

"Goodbye," I manage, my throat tight as they slip into the deepening twilight, swallowed by the festival lights and the shadows beyond.

I stand there long after they vanish, the warmth leaving my cheeks and cold settling in my bones. I cover my eyes with my hands, trying not to cry, trying not to let the fear and sorrow overwhelm me. The laughter, the music, the festival all feel distant now, and I feel completely alone.

Taking a deep breath, I force myself to think clearly. There has to be a way for me to earn some money. Even though there aren't many jobs for women in this time, there must be something I can do without selling myself. Maybe the man I met earlier, Marcus, would be willing to help me find work. He seems kind, and he's clearly a high-ranking and wealthy man. If I could find a task to do for him, I might be able to repay Flavia, Sabina, and Tullia for their hospitality and everything they've shared with me.

I move through the crowd, scanning the square for Marcus. I look around the forum at each person moving through the square—a living echo of the past I've studied. I'm so thankful I chose to learn their ancient language so I can understand the lyrics of each song and the playful chatter of the children running past me. A pang of helplessness strikes me. So many of these people will die if no one warns them before the mountain erupts.

I wander over to a large crowd watching a religious ceremony. The priestesses are honoring Venus and Jupiter, their voices rising in a haunting chant: *"Prosperitas et abundantia, dona nobis, dii!"* For prosperity and abundance, they pray. It's frustrating and upsetting to know how little time they have left.

Marcus. He's attending to the priestesses in a way that clearly matters, and I pause to watch him for a moment. He's serious, engaged, and I can tell he notices everything. Even from a distance, it's clear how focused he is and how much he cares about his work. As he bends to lift an altar off the ground, moving it to the other side of the platform, he radiates confident masculine energy, and his dark hair and eyes are just…dreamy.

Embarrassment overwhelms me when he looks my way and

catches me watching him. My face heats up, but he doesn't seem bothered. He smiles warmly, and a thrill runs through me. He waves and motions for me to stay where I am, and that he'll be over in a moment. I wait until he steps aside from the ceremonial duties and makes his way toward me.

As Marcus walks over, I try to remind myself not to say anything too forward or flirtatious. This man is from two thousand years in *my* past, and yet, I'm so attracted to him that when he smiles, I almost forget everything I was just telling myself.

"Fiona, thank you for waiting," he says.

"Of course," I reply. "I know you're working, and I know you're busy, but… I was wondering if I could speak with you somewhere more private?"

He glances toward the ceremonial crowd and then back at me. "I'm almost done with my work for the night. Once I finish here, would you like to join me for a late dinner at the tavern?"

"Yes," I manage to say. I can feel the tension draining, replaced by anticipation. "I'd like that very much. Thank you."

He nods. "Wait here. I'll return as soon as I finish."

I smile and nod, and he walks back toward the ceremony, Felix at his heels. I sit down on the nearby temple steps, trying to figure out what I will say to this incredibly sexy man from ancient Pompeii over dinner.

A little while later, Marcus and Felix return. "We'll drop my dog off at my house before heading to the tavern," he says.

"Perfect," I reply, and the three of us start walking through the dark streets. The festival fades behind us, and I can't stop sneaking glances at Marcus.

When we arrive at his house, I'm awestruck by its beauty. From the courtyard, I can see the elegant, structured lines I've only ever known as ruins and debris beneath layers of ash. It's a strange place to stand, balanced between envy and regret. He is clearly a very wealthy man, living in a luxurious home, and I find myself envying the mosaic tiles beneath my feet, the fountain, the fruit trees and bushes, and the flower gardens. Yet, the feeling is quickly swallowed by grief, knowing that soon, all of it will be buried.

Marcus opens the door, pauses at the threshold, and calls into the house, "Aurelia?"

A moment later, a servant girl appears in the doorway, an oil lamp in her hand.

"Please take Felix inside," Marcus says. "And make sure he's fed."

"Yes, Dominus," she replies, bending to usher the dog inside before disappearing back through the doorway.

Marcus turns back to me once the door closes. "Are you ready?" he asks.

"I am," I reply.

He smiles. "Are you hungry?"

"I am very hungry," I say, and this time I don't bother to try to hide my grin.

"Good," he says, gesturing toward the street. "Come. The tavern isn't far."

We head back into the street together, the distant sounds of the festival still echoing through the night. When we reach the tavern and step inside, the shift is immediate—cool night air is replaced by smoke from the hearth and the noise of the crowded room. Tables are packed close together, people leaning in to talk to one another while servers move quickly between them, balancing trays of food and wine as they go.

Marcus guides me through the room with an ease that tells me he's a regular here. Finally, we find an open table near the back. He gestures for me to sit, and I lower myself onto the chair across from him.

A barmaid approaches, wiping her hands on her apron. "What can I bring you, Dominus?"

Marcus orders for both of us. "Please bring us lamb, bread, cheese, and your finest wine."

She nods. "I'll bring it shortly."

As she disappears into the crowd, he turns his attention back to me, studying me in a way that makes my heartbeat speed up. "Earlier today you said you were from the north," he says. "What part?"

I hesitate, choosing my words carefully. I can't tell him too much, but I don't want to lie to him, either. "Farther than most people from here have ever traveled," I say at last. "Beyond Rome. It's much colder there."

His brow lifts, intrigued. "And what brings you all the way to Italia?"

"Curiosity," I say, smiling. "I wanted to see more of the world."

"That is not something many women can afford to do alone," he says, though there's no judgment in his tone—only interest.

"I wasn't alone at first, but I've learned to manage," I reply.

"I believe that." He gives me an encouraging nod.

The barmaid returns, setting down cups of honeyed wine and a platter of food between us.

Marcus thanks her and gestures to the food. "Let's eat."

I don't need to be told twice. I tear off a piece of bread, trying to keep my manners in check as I take a bite.

"You travel far, manage on your own, and yet you say very little about yourself," he says, watching me over the rim of his cup. I swallow, meeting his gaze. "Should I be worried?"

"Only if you think I look dangerous."

He smiles at that, unmistakably amused. "Not dangerous," he says. "But definitely very interesting."

Another blush creeps into my cheeks, and I look down into my wineglass. For a moment, the noise of the tavern wraps around us while I muster the courage, trying to find the words I came here for.

"Marcus," I begin, "I was actually hoping to ask you something rather important."

He looks up immediately. "Of course."

"I was wondering if you might know of any work I could do… just for a few days. Enough to earn a little money."

He leans back in his chair, considering my request. "Are you traveling through and have simply run out of coin?"

"Yes," I say, grateful for the simplicity of the inquiry. "That's exactly it."

Marcus stares into my eyes for a moment before he asks, "I don't mean to pry, and I ask only out of concern, but do you have somewhere to stay tonight, Fiona?"

I realize I don't actually know where my friends are right now or how I'd even find my way back to their room from here without them. The thought stings, and I have no choice but to admit the truth. I shake my head. "No… I don't have anywhere to stay tonight."

The admission leaves me exposed in a way I can't take back, and I brace myself for his reaction.

"Don't worry," he says, a soft kindness in his voice. "We'll figure something out."

I look at him with gratitude in my heart. The people of this city are different. They're warm, caring, accepting of strangers, and most of all, they deserve a chance to live long, happy, and peaceful lives. I've got to find a way to save them—especially him.

12

GLADIATORS

MARCUS

I watch Fiona across the table as she finishes the last of her meal, still trying to understand what she's told me about herself. There are so many things about her that don't quite make sense to me yet. She speaks carefully, as though each word is planned before it leaves her lips, yet there is nothing guarded in her eyes when she looks at me. That contradiction draws my attention more than I intend.

"You are quite mysterious," I say.

She gives me an uncertain smile. "Am I?"

"Yes," I reply, setting my glass down. "And I'm very interested in getting to learn more about you, if you'll permit me the honor."

She lowers her gaze briefly and then looks back up at me. There's something so different about her. I've never met—or even *seen* for that matter—anyone quite like her before. I find myself speaking again before I fully decide to. "Fiona... would you like to stay in my guest bedroom tonight? You'll be safe and comfortable there."

She pauses, perhaps in surprise, followed by consideration. "Are you certain? I have no way to repay you."

"I'm certain, and you'd owe me nothing. It would not be proper to send you wandering the streets at this hour without knowing where you'll sleep. I have many servants, several of them female, so I assure you, we will not be alone."

She looks at me with those big blue eyes for a moment longer, and then nods. "I would appreciate that. Thank you, Marcus."

"Of course," I reply.

We finish what remains of the food and wine, and I signal the barmaid to settle the bill. Leaving the tavern behind, we step into the dark streets, and I walk beside her, close enough to protect her from anyone who might be up to no good at this late hour.

After a moment, I ask her another question, hoping I'm not being too intrusive. "Fiona?" I begin.

"Yes?"

"Were you able to speak with the priest of Venus yesterday morning? Did he help you?"

She looks down for a moment, her expression somber, and when she speaks, her voice loses its usual confidence. "No... he wasn't able to help."

"I see. I'm very sorry he could not assist you."

She nods, but the disappointment remains in her expression. "Thank you."

"I hope," I continue, "that I may eventually be able to help you with whatever it is you're seeking."

She looks at me then, a sliver of hope returning to her gorgeous face. "Thank you, Marcus. That's kind of you to say."

I nod. "Of course. It's simply the truth."

We reach my house, and I open the door. Felix immediately runs in our direction, tail wagging excitedly as he approaches us.

"Good evening, Felix," I say, scratching behind his ears. "I hope you were a good boy while I was gone."

Fiona laughs and crouches beside him, reaching out to pet him, too. Felix leans into her touch, his tail thumping against the floor. "You're quite the charmer, aren't you?" she says.

I grin and offer her a hand to help her up. "He's got a soft spot for anyone who'll give him attention or food."

I lead her further inside, gesturing toward the guest room. "This is it," I say. "It's simple but comfortable."

She looks around, taking in the room. "It's more than I expected," she says. "Thank you so much for your hospitality."

"You're more than welcome here," I reply, looking at her and wondering what it would be like to kiss her perfect lips. Shaking the thought off quickly before I do something foolish, I ask, "Is there anything more I can do for you tonight?"

"Oh, Marcus, you've already done too much. No, thank you."

I nod. "Goodnight, Fiona."

"Goodnight, Marcus." Her gaze lingers for a moment longer than I expect. After a moment, she enters the room, and I leave her there, closing the door quietly behind me.

"Felix," I call softly, and my dog trots over. I pat his head before heading to my room, and he follows me, as always, curling up on the floor beside my bed.

I strip off my clothes as my mind races. I keep thinking about Fiona. I can't shake the way she looked at me earlier, the mix of confidence and caution in her eyes. I've met countless women, but she's unlike any of them.

I lie in bed, the house dark and silent, but sleep doesn't come. I keep picturing her smile—the way it genuinely lit up her entire face. I wonder if she feels out of place here, in a city that's so far from her home. I can't help but feel protective of her and try to imagine how I can make her feel more at ease and more at home.

I close my eyes, but the image of her doesn't fade. It stays with me, and soon, I fall asleep, thoughts of Fiona filling my dreams.

THE SUN'S JUST STARTING TO RISE WHEN I WAKE UP. FELIX IS ON THE floor beside the bed, lifting his head to look at me like he knows it's time to get moving. I rub my eyes and sit up, trying to shake off the sleep. My thoughts immediately land on Fiona. I wonder if she's awake.

I hear a soft knock at the door. "Dominus?" Aurelia's voice

calls out.

"Come in," I reply.

"Dominus," she says, "would you like me to invite your guest to your breakfast table?"

I nod. "Yes, please."

She bows and leaves.

I get out of bed, stretch, dress quickly, and head for the table. Felix follows, looking up at me, waiting for his breakfast.

I sit down at the table, and a few minutes later, Fiona walks in. She looks refreshed and very pretty this morning, even though she's still in last night's clothing. She's pinned her hair up, the pale, almost white, curls gathered at the top of her head.

"Good morning," she says.

"Good morning," I reply, getting up to pull out the chair for her. "Did you sleep well?"

"I did, thank you," she says, settling into the chair. She glances around at the table. "You have a stunningly beautiful home."

"Thank you," I say. "I'm glad you're comfortable."

She picks up some bread that Aurelia has set out for the table, dipping it into the oil. Felix immediately sits at her feet, watching her every move.

"You can give him some, if you want," I say. "He always thinks he's starving."

Fiona laughs, breaking off a piece of the bread and feeding it to him. "I guess he's spoiled."

"Very spoiled," I say with a laugh.

Aurelia steps in with the plates, setting them down carefully in front of us. The eggs are perfectly cooked, still warm and steaming. She places a small bowl of olives beside each plate and leaves the bread within reach. "Is there anything else, Dominus?" she asks, looking between us.

"No, thank you, Aurelia," I reply. "This is wonderful."

Aurelia bows and leaves the room.

As Fiona and I eat our breakfast, I go over my plans for the day in my head.

"Fiona," I say, glancing at her. "Would you like to join me at the festival today?"

She looks up from her plate, her eyes meeting mine. "I'd love that," she says softly. "But I know you'll be busy. Will you be distracted if I tag along?"

"I'll be working most of the time, but the gladiator match is this afternoon. You're welcome to join me if you wish."

She smiles, a touch of relief in her expression. "Thank you. I'd enjoy that."

By the time we finish breakfast, it's time to leave. I turn to Felix, who's sitting beside my leg under the table.

"Stay here, and be a good boy today for Aurelia, Felix. We will see you tonight." I pat his head. He whines but doesn't stand when I step away. Turning to Fiona, I ask, "Shall we?"

She nods, and we leave the house. The walk is relatively quiet, though I do point out a few buildings she may need to be aware of while she's in the city. She smiles and notes lovely flowers and other parts of nature I often overlook.

When we reach the forum, I'm not surprised that it's already packed with merchants and festival-goers, all bustling about in preparation for the day's events. Today, there will be games, performances, and later, the gladiator matches at the amphitheater.

I see Quintus near a cluster of traders and make my way over to him, Fiona by my side. He's speaking with a merchant, his attention on the exchange, but when he sees me, his face brightens.

"Marcus!" Quintus greets me, his voice easily heard over the noise of the crowd. "Glad to see you've made it this morning. Busy day ahead, eh?"

I nod, pointing to Fiona beside me. "Quintus, this is Fiona," I say.

My friend shifts his attention to her, offering a friendly smile. "It's a pleasure, Fiona. I'm Quintus."

Fiona smiles back. "The pleasure is mine."

"Quintus is my right-hand man," I explain. "He's also my greatest friend, and perhaps later, you'll meet his lovely wife and rambunctious children."

"I would love to meet them." Her face brightens with genuine enthusiasm.

"They will be here around lunchtime, as usual. You must join us for the noon meal, Fiona. But for now, I'm needed at the livestock market. I'll see the two of you shortly." Quintus waves and walks away.

Fiona and I both wave to him as he hurries off to attend to business, and I look over at her. "Would you like to help me with the priest of Jupiter's ceremonial altars? I've got to move them from the temple to the shrine near the fountain."

"I would love to help," she replies, smiling.

The morning passes quickly as Fiona helps me with the priest of Jupiter's altars and other tasks around the forum. By midday, we take a break and sit down for lunch with Quintus and his family. The meal is quick but pleasant, and Fiona clearly enjoys the company of Cornelia and the children.

Afterward, I nod toward the amphitheater in the distance. "It's time for the matches," I say. "Shall we?"

She nods. "Yes, let's."

Fiona and I make our way through the streets toward the amphitheater. The roar of the crowd is deafening as we enter, and the air is thick with anticipation. The gladiators are being led into the arena, their weapons gleaming under the bright midday sun.

We take our seats and I look over at her beside me, noticing the way she's holding herself—a little too tense, eyes filled with curiosity—and I wonder if they even have gladiator matches in the north where she's from.

The first match begins, and the energy shifts in the air, the crowd cheering as two gladiators circle each other, their swords raised. Fiona flinches at the first clash, and I catch the unease that passes over her face. I reach out instinctively, placing a hand on her shoulder. "Are you all right?" I ask, keeping my voice calm, though I'm starting to feel her discomfort even more intensely.

She nods. "I'm fine," she says, but her voice wavers, betraying her.

The match intensifies as one of the gladiators is knocked to the ground, and the crowd erupts in cheers. Fiona stiffens beside me, her breath quickening. She turns her head away from the arena, yet I can tell she's still listening, even if she's trying to avoid it.

"You don't have to stay if you're not comfortable," I say quietly, leaning in close so only she can hear.

But she shakes her head, her gaze returning to the fight, though it's clear she's not enjoying it in the least. "No, it's fine." Her voice is strained, her jaw set tightly.

The gladiators clash again, and this time, one of them is knocked unconscious, blood staining the sand. The crowd goes wild. That's when I notice Fiona's hands are clenched tightly at her sides, her knuckles white. Her jaw tightens even more, her eyes fixed on the arena.

When they release the lion into the ring, Fiona stands, her breath coming in short, uneven gasps. "I can't watch this." Her voice trembles with each word.

Before I can say anything, she pushes through our row and heads toward the steps leading to the exit.

I follow her, calling her name over the noise, but she doesn't slow down or even turn around. Finally, I catch up to her, resting my hand on her arm gently, not enough to stop her, but enough to pull her attention back to me. "Fiona," I say softly. "Let's leave."

She looks up at me, eyes brimming with tears. "I'm sorry, Marcus. It's just that I've never seen anything like that before. I should've known what to expect, but honestly, I just didn't understand how violent and brutal this would be." Her voice quivers.

"You don't need to apologize," I reply, taking a step closer. "I didn't realize it was your first match. I should've warned you. Let's get you out of here."

As we walk away from the amphitheater, I can't help but think about her deep feelings of empathy. Who is this woman with such a soft heart, so gentle and kind in a world that is anything but? It's like she doesn't belong in this place. She's not hardened by the brutality around us, and I can't help but be drawn to that while wondering how she's remained so innocent and pure.

13

WHAT HE'S MISSING

FIONA

I run out of the amphitheater entrance and stop to catch my breath. Tears come faster than I expect, running hot down my cheeks, and I try to swallow the lump in my throat before Marcus sees just how upset I truly am. I don't want to seem too soft or like I come from a more progressive era because I don't want to blow my cover, but the gladiator games upset me more than I realized they would.

My eyes keep burning as I try to wipe the tears off my face before he catches up to me. The arena still feels too close. I look around, frantic, and all I see are soldiers and civilians, but I can't shake the feeling that the massive Barbary lion has followed me out here.

I didn't realize attending the games would affect me so strongly. I've read textbooks and firsthand accounts, and I've seen all the movies about gladiators—everything from *Spartacus* to *Gladiator II* with Paul Mescal—but seeing it up close in real life is completely different. I just got so caught up spending time with Marcus and didn't even think about it before I agreed to go in there. Feeling the dread of loss, seeing the fear of death in people's eyes... I couldn't handle it.

Footsteps slow behind me, and I know Marcus is there before he even speaks. "Fiona, are you all right?" he asks.

I turn to face him, trying to answer normally, but my voice comes out shaky, anyway. "I'm fine. I'm sorry. I didn't expect to feel this way."

He steps closer. I can tell from the way his eyes are searching my face that he's trying to read me, and to figure out what he's missing. "Was it the violence? The fighting?" he asks.

"It isn't just the fighting," I say. "Marcus, do you realize that if they keep doing this with those animals, some of the species won't be around much longer?"

Marcus frowns slightly. "What do you mean?"

I hesitate because I can hear how silly it sounds in my head, but I say it anyway. "I mean, they're destroying them. Hunting them for these games, using them in ways they can't recover from. The elephants from North Africa, the Barbary lions, the Atlas bears, and the Caspian tigers are all at risk of disappearing."

For a moment, he doesn't respond, his handsome sun-bronzed face turning a shade or three paler and his lips pressing into a thin line. And I haven't even mentioned the horrors and atrocities they do to the human men in those rings. I don't need to wonder what kind of empathy I would stir in Marcus's heart if I pointed that out through a modern lens, and I don't think I have to. I believe he understands.

"I never thought of it that way," he admits quietly. "Please forgive me for bringing you here, Fiona."

"You don't have to apologize," I reply.

"How can I make it up to you?" he asks, taking both my hands in his. "We can go anywhere you want. Just name the place."

"I'm not familiar enough with your city to know where to go," I admit.

In reality, there really isn't anywhere that sounds enjoyable to me in this era. The bathhouses don't appeal to me—they seem like a breeding ground for infection. I've already been to the tavern with Marcus, and it was a bit too noisy for my liking. Right now, the forum is incredibly busy because of the festival, and I got assaulted in the temple and kicked out of there, so I never want to go back.

We both look around for a moment, the streets still bustling and growing even more crowded as the sun starts to set, light sliding over the carved stone buildings around us. Even now, I'm thinking about the amphitheater and the way I didn't really understand how massive it is until I was standing right outside. I look up at its walls, carved into the city in that perfect oval, rows stacked into the structure like it was grown out of the ground instead of built on it. And the buildings here still have those upper edges and squared cutouts along the tops. I stare in awe at the details that I've only ever seen in ruins and paintings before now.

"Why don't I take you home and have a proper meal prepared for you before we return to the festival this evening?" Marcus asks.

It feels like it should be getting close to dinnertime, and I'd really like to see more of Marcus's beautiful home. "I'd appreciate that," I reply. "Thank you."

We walk away from the amphitheater toward his house. In this part of the city, the houses are still well-built but smaller and less ornate than the ones in Marcus's district. The farther we go, the shabbier they become, and then I start to recognize the neighborhood. When I see the fountain where Flavia and I drew water, I know exactly where we are.

I slow down. "Marcus... would you mind if I stopped here for a moment? I just want to check on some friends. I haven't seen them since yesterday, and I want to make sure they're all right."

He doesn't question it. "Of course. I'll come with you."

We turn down the street I remember. The house is there, and we approach. I hesitate only a second before stepping forward and knocking.

After a moment, the door opens, and Tullia is standing there. Her eyes light up with relief and joy. She steps forward and pulls me into a hug. "Fiona, we were wondering if you would ever come back!" she nearly shouts at me.

Tullia lets go of me just as I hear a voice from inside. "Is that Fiona?"

A second later, Flavia and Sabina appear in the doorway and rush over, pulling me into a group hug. "Are you all right?" Flavia asks.

"I'm fine," I tell them, laughing as they finally let go of me. "Let me introduce you to my new friend—this is Marcus. Marcus, these are Tullia, Flavia, and Sabina."

He inclines his head. "It's a pleasure to meet you. I'm Marcus Valerius."

Tullia's face brightens with recognition. "We've seen you before—you're the man with the beautiful dog."

"The massive, beautiful dog," Flavia adds.

Sabina steps a little closer, studying him. "Have you been taking good care of our Fiona?" she asks.

Marcus hesitates, clearly unsure how to answer, and Sabina laughs.

"I'm not serious. We can see that you have."

"Yes," Tullia adds with a teasing smile. "It's quite obvious."

"All right," I cut in, trying to save him from any more of their taunting. "Leave Marcus alone. We only stopped by to let you know I'm safe—and that I'm in good hands."

Flavia nods. "We appreciate you bringing her by. Would you mind if we spoke with her alone for a moment?"

"Of course," Marcus says.

I give him a smile and a wave before letting them pull me inside, the door closing behind us.

Inside the room, Flavia speaks first. "Fiona, we didn't know where you were—we were terrified! You can't tell us Vesuvius is going to erupt and then give us nothing else. We didn't know if we'd ever see you again. Tell us the exact day—when does it happen?" she asks, the words tumbling out in a rush.

"I'm so sorry. I didn't know how to get back here, and I had no idea where you were. August twenty-fourth," I say. "That's when it happens."

"What should we do, Fiona?" Sabina asks.

"Leave," I say. "As soon as you can. Just go. Go to Neapolis, Roma, Capua, or Puteoli. Anywhere but here. Take what you can carry—money, valuables, anything sentimental—and get out before the twenty-fourth. If you can leave tonight, even better."

Flavia looks me in the eye. "You're certain?"

"Yes," I say. "I'm certain."

"We leave tonight," Tullia says, looking from Flavia to Sabina. Both women nod and begin packing.

"Are you coming with us?" Sabina asks me.

I glance toward the doorway, my thoughts immediately going to Marcus. "No. I'm staying. I can't leave yet, but I *will* get out. I promise."

Tullia nods, grabs a satchel, and moves over to her wardrobe. "Fiona, before you leave, let me give you a fresh tunic."

I take it from her. "Thank you, Tullia," I say. "I don't know how I could ever repay all of you." Holding the fresh, clean tunic in my hands, I think about how I haven't bathed or changed clothes in far too long. A tear wells up in my eye, and I feel silly for getting emotional over something so small.

"You've paid us plenty. You're saving our lives," Tullia says, pulling me into another hug.

Flavia and Sabina join us, and the four of us stand there, holding each other—brought together by one secret we share, while the rest of the city remains in the dark.

"I should go," I say, wiping the tear away. "I'm going to try to get everyone out of the city."

Flavia squeezes my hand, and I throw the tunic over my shoulder, walking back out the door and closing it behind me.

I step back outside and see Marcus standing nearby. As I approach, he meets my eyes with a small, questioning look. "Is everything all right?" he asks.

I nod, smiling. "Yes, everything's fine."

"Shall we?" He tilts his head toward the road, grinning.

"Lead the way," I reply.

We walk through the rough part of town, past the crumbling buildings and narrow alleys where the air is thick with dust and noise.

Marcus glances at me. "What shall we have for dinner?"

"You should allow your cook to decide," I reply.

He chuckles, shaking his head. "Of course you'd say that."

I give him a teasing look. "I don't mind as long as I don't have to choose."

Soon, the chaos starts to fade, the noise lessens, the buildings become sturdier, and the air is much cleaner. We're reaching the nicer part of the city now, where the streets are wider and the houses taller, their gardens neatly kept.

As we walk, I think about how good it would feel to wash my hair and finally get the last few days of grime off my skin. Then I think about how awkward and embarrassing it would be to ask someone as attractive as Marcus if I could use his bathtub. I need to muster the courage before we get to his house.

"Marcus," I finally say. "I have a strange question for you."

"You can ask me anything, Fiona," he replies.

"When we arrive… could I bathe?"

He looks over at me at once.

"Of course," he says easily. "I'll have Aurelia draw you a bath."

"Thank you," I reply, smiling at him. "I genuinely appreciate your hospitality and companionship," I add, trying not to blush.

"I appreciate your company as well, Fiona. I've never met anyone like you," he replies.

As his garden comes into view, I can't help but admire the well-kept bushes, colorful flowers, and the neat rows of plants.

Marcus opens the door, and as we step inside, Felix comes running toward us. I bend down to greet him, scratching behind his ears. Then a woman comes into the room and stops when she sees us. "Welcome home, Dominus," she says to Marcus.

"Good evening, Aurelia," Marcus says. "Would you mind drawing a bath for Fiona, please?"

"Of course," she replies, bowing and motioning for me to follow.

As I follow Aurelia past the kitchen, I hear Marcus step inside and say, "Callista, please prepare whatever you decide for our dinner tonight. I have a guest, and she has asked that you choose the menu."

I laugh quietly as Aurelia leads me into the bathing room, where the large tub takes up most of the space. She gestures toward it and back at me. "I'll be back shortly. I need to fetch water from the well."

I nod, but as she turns to leave, I feel a sudden impulse to help. I step toward the door, and Aurelia looks at me, a little surprised.

"I can help carry the water," I offer.

She pauses and then gives me a smile. "That's very kind of you. I'd appreciate the help."

I set Tullia's clean tunic on the stool near the tub and follow Aurelia outside to the well. We fill two large buckets with water, carrying them back to the bathing room. Then, we repeat our steps until the tub is full.

When we're done, Aurelia moves back, looking at me. "Thank you for your help," she says, her tone warm.

"No, thank you," I say.

"Here are some oils and perfumed salts," she says, handing me a small clay jar and a cloth. "I'll leave you to your bath."

I nod, grateful for her help, and she heads for the door, leaving me alone to bathe. The water is warm, thanks to the hypocaust system Marcus is rich enough to have in his home, and I sigh as I lower myself into the tub. It's nothing like the hot showers I'm used to back home, but it's still a relief. I sink deeper, feeling the culture shock of the last few days begin to lift as I let the water soothe my tired body.

I scrub away the dirt and sweat of Pompeii's streets. With each movement, the water grows clouded with grime.

I close my eyes for a moment, the sound of the water lapping against the sides of the tub calming my racing thoughts. I can't believe I'm still here. I'm still stuck in a world that isn't mine—a city that's destined for tragedy.

I step out, dry off with the towel Aurelia left for me, and slip into the tunic. Taking a deep breath, I walk over to the bronze mirror on the wall to braid my hair.

Now, I have to face Marcus over dinner, and I dread what I have to tell him. I need to convince him that Vesuvius is going to erupt, and he has the power and connections to help save lives. Together, we could make a difference, but how do I bring it up without the risk of sounding insane?

14

RETRIBUTION

Marcus

I'm sitting at the dining room table with Felix at my heel, waiting for Fiona, when I hear footsteps in the hallway. I stand out of respect when she enters the room, but when I see her—fresh from the bath, hair braided, wearing a clean tunic—I can't take my eyes off her.

I step toward her and help her into her chair. "You look radiant tonight," I say.

"Thank you," she replies, settling into the seat across from mine, a place rarely filled.

As I walk back around to my side of the table, I find myself thinking about how nice it is to have a guest—and how fortunate I am that this particular guest is both intriguing and beautiful.

I take my seat just as Aurelia enters with a tray holding my best bottle of wine, two glasses, and two plates of food.

"Thank you, Aurelia," I say.

"Yes, thank you so much," Fiona adds.

Aurelia bows her head and leaves us to our meal.

I pour the wine and set the bottle aside before looking up at Fiona. "I saw you helping Aurelia carrying water from the well earlier."

A flush rises in her cheeks. "You saw that?"

"I did. I would've helped you both, but I was getting a thorn out of Felix's paw. Although, Fiona, I was curious, why were you helping with that? You're my guest—you don't need to assist the servants."

Fiona shrugs her shoulders. "If I can help someone, I will. It doesn't matter who they are or what the task is."

I take in the meaning of her words and find myself even more intrigued than I was before. She isn't just stunningly beautiful; she is also kind and thoughtful. She thinks about the servants and even the wild animals as though they are just as deserving of protection, help, or comfort as anyone else, and even though I agree with her, I realize I have never truly thought about things in that way. I find myself wondering who this woman is that I have had the pleasure of meeting, the one who is turning my views upside down, or perhaps right side up.

"If I may be so bold as to ask, why did you suggest letting the cook choose the meal?"

"I thought she would choose something fairly simple," Fiona says. "I hoped she'd choose a dish that was easy to make and easy to clean up afterward."

Her answer makes me more certain of what I already see in her— that she is not just kind occasionally, but consistently so, in a way that changes how she sees the world around her.

I pull off a piece of quail and feed it to Felix under the table. He swallows it whole. Looking back at Fiona, I ask, "Would you still like to accompany me to the festival after dinner? I completely understand if you're tired and would like to stay and rest, but I would love to have you be my guest this evening."

"Of course, Marcus. I would love to go," she replies. She sets her fork down and looks at me with a more serious expression. "Although, I do need to tell you something important…and it's going to sound odd."

"You can tell me anything," I say. "I'd love to know more about you."

She starts to speak, but there's a knock on the door.

I glance toward it, then back to her. "Will you excuse me one moment?"

I stand to answer the door and, as I walk, I'm wondering who it could be at this hour when most people are already at the festival. My thoughts go to Quintus before I can stop them and to the possibility that something has gone wrong at the forum. I've been home while something I could have prevented was happening.

I open the door and find a boy—no more than twelve—standing there with a terrified look on his face. "It's your brother! It's Lucius! Come quick!"

Before I can answer him, I hear Fiona behind me, rushing over. We follow the boy as he turns and runs down the street.

As we run, I think about Fiona behind me. This isn't something she should be caught up in, and I wish she had stayed behind, but I already know enough about her to realize she isn't the kind of woman who hears someone is in trouble and turns away.

"What happened?" I yell to the boy.

"Lucius owes gambling debts! They came for him!"

"What are they doing to him?" I call out as we run.

"They're beating him," the boy says, breathless as he keeps going. "They said if he doesn't pay, they're going to tie him to the back of a horse and drag him through the festival parade tonight. Said everyone will see what happens when you don't pay."

I hear shouting, and I know we're close. Rage rips through me, and I fear Fiona is about to see me at my worst.

When we reach the alley where the thugs have my brother cornered, I look at Fiona and the boy. "Both of you, keep running," I order. "Get to the forum and find Quintus—he'll be near where the parade is being set up at the temple steps. Tell him to bring men and come here now."

They don't argue. The boy nods, taking off again, and Fiona follows him.

I sprint down the alley to see Lucius pinned against the wall again, a man driving blow after blow into his stomach.

My knife is in my hand before I reach them. One of the men turns as I close the distance, his sword coming up too late. I drive into him hard, cutting into his ribs and twisting through the motion until he drops against the wall and slides down it. Lucius is still trapped between the others.

Someone swings at me, and I sidestep his blade, but it's close enough to feel the movement of it past me. I bury my knife into his stomach. He folds forward with a sharp gasp and stumbles back, collapsing.

Another lets go of Lucius, reaching for his sword, but I grab him by the front of his tunic and slam him into the wall so hard his head snaps back. Before he can recover, I drive my knife into his shoulder.

Shouting behind me grows louder, footsteps flooding the alley. I glance back to see Quintus and the men he could round up on their way here.

I drive my knife into the side of another man, spinning him to the ground, when I feel Quintus right beside me. Our friends take down more attackers as the alley explodes with chaos.

I duck under a wild swing and land a strike with my knife to the thigh, pushing the man back into the wall. He screams, and before he can recover, one of our men steps in, knocking him down with a fist to the gut.

When another man charges at me, I sidestep and grab him by the throat, slamming him against the wall hard. I sink my knife into his throat, and he goes limp, collapsing in a heap.

As I catch my breath, Quintus and our friends cut through the remaining attackers. When they're all either dead or have run away, I glance over at Lucius. Fiona is cradling his head in one arm, applying pressure to a chest wound with her other hand. She looks up at me. "We need to get him home. Fast."

I look at Fiona while wiping the blood off my knife before slipping it back into its sheath and manage a small smile before I lock eyes with Quintus. "I owe you."

Quintus gives a quick nod. "That's what friends are for. Don't worry about the festival tonight—I've got it under control. Just go take care of your brother. We'll clean this mess up."

I nod again. "I will. Thank you, Quintus."

Fiona and I help Lucius to his feet. He's shaky, but he can walk. We lead him out of the alley and into the street.

I see the boy who came to find me, his eyes filled with horror. We stop in front of him. "What's your name, puer?"

"Decimus, Dominus," he answers, his voice trembling.

I look at Decimus. "You were very brave and did the right thing," I say. "You helped when it mattered most."

Fiona nods in agreement. "It took a lot of courage. You should be proud of yourself."

Decimus nods, a little more confident now, but his eyes still carry the significance of the moment.

"Follow us, Decimus," I say, my curiosity piqued. "How did you know where to find me?"

He walks next to us. "Everyone knows where you live, Dominus."

I'm a little surprised by his answer. "I didn't think anyone kept track of that," I mutter, more to myself than to him.

We walk slowly down the street, Lucius leaning heavily on both Fiona and me. Each movement is painful for him, and the weight of his body makes every step a struggle. Decimus follows behind us.

When my house finally comes into view, the sight of it brings a small sense of relief, though I know this night is far from over. Lucius is barely conscious and he needs help—right away.

We reach the door, and I push it open. "Aurelia!" I call out, the urgency sharp in my voice.

Felix hears the door open and immediately trots over to greet me. His tail wags as he approaches, but when he sees Lucius leaning on us, barely standing, his demeanor shifts. Felix's ears prick up, and his wagging slows to a stop. He sniffs the air and takes a step back, sensing the danger of the situation.

"Aurelia!" I call again.

She appears quickly, her eyes filling with concern and dismay when she sees Lucius, bleeding and injured, struggling to stay on his feet. "What happened?" she asks, her voice tight with concern.

"He's been badly beaten again," I say, my voice clipped. "I'm putting him in my bed, Aurelia. We need to tend to him."

Fiona and I help Lucius down the hall, his body heavy against mine as we move him toward my room. Once inside, I guide him to the bed and help him lie down.

Aurelia returns a moment later with clean cloths, salves, and bandages in hand, ready to help. She steps to Lucius's side, her eyes scanning his injuries. "We need to clean him up first," she murmurs, using a damp cloth to carefully wipe blood from his face.

Fiona kneels beside him, pressing another cloth to his chest. "We'll need to stop the bleeding as quickly as possible. Aurelia, do you have any yarrow?" she asks, looking at the wound.

Aurelia nods and hurries out of the room. She returns moments later with a bundle of dried herbs, handing them to Fiona.

Fiona presses the yarrow into Lucius's wound, and after a few moments, the bleeding begins to slow. She looks up. "It's stopping."

I watch the women work, and I think about Fiona and how courageous it was for her to follow me into that alley, not knowing what she was getting herself into. I see now that she's knowledgeable, able to handle what's needed in tough situations, and she's the most selfless person I've ever met.

After a few moments, I step away, needing air. I move toward the front door and open it. Outside, I see Decimus sitting on the steps, Felix resting his head in his lap. The boy is stroking the dog's fur, and for a moment, the peaceful scene nearly makes me forget about tonight's trouble. Decimus reminds me of Lucius at that age, and I feel a lump in my throat, thinking about how much I love my younger brother.

"Decimus," I say, and the boy looks up at me. "Thank you for your help tonight, puer."

"Of course, Dominus."

"If you ever need anything—anything at all—come and find me."

"I will, Dominus," he replies.

"I'll arrange for a chaperone to take you home in my carriage. Does that sound good to you?" I ask the boy.

He looks up at me, nodding gratefully. "Thank you, Dominus."

I give him a nod before stepping back inside the house. I find Aurelia in the hallway, carrying a few more cloths.

"Aurelia," I say, taking the cloths from her. "Please find Titus and have him take the boy waiting outside home in the carriage."

She nods and hurries off. I walk toward the room to check on Lucius. Inside the room, I move to the bed, setting the clean cloths next to him on the table. The bleeding has stopped, and Fiona and Aurelia have done well to clean Lucius up, but my heart aches at the sight of my younger brother in such pain.

"Marcus," Fiona says. "Don't worry. He's going to make it."

"Thank you," I whisper, "for all your help tonight."

"Of course," she says, rising and walking over to me. "Are you hurt?" She looks me over.

"No, I just have a few scratches and perhaps a bruise or two, but I'm fine," I reply.

She stands in front of me, and I look into her sapphire eyes while holding back the urge to stroke her face. She seems to feel what's building between us, too, because her cheeks turn a deep pink.

"I've never seen anyone fight like that," she says softly.

"I'm sorry, Fiona. I know how you feel about violence." I take a deep breath and look away.

She lifts a hand and gently presses her finger to my lips. "That wasn't violence," she says. "That was retribution."

15

COURAGEOUS

FIONA

I wake to the first streams of orange and yellow blazing through the window of the guest room in Marcus's house, but I have no idea how I got here. I rub my eyes and try to remember going to bed, forcing myself to think back through the events of the night. I remember the fight and the way Marcus stepped in to protect his brother from being killed. I remember bringing Lucius back here and helping tend to his wounds late into the night. But I don't remember getting into this bed....

I frown and get out of bed, trying to work out the missing pieces. There's a cloth, a clay basin, a cup, a pitcher of water, and a small dish of crushed herbs and salt sitting on a small wooden table by the wall. I pour water into the basin and rinse my face with the cool water. Then I take the crushed herbs and salt from the dish and rub them over my teeth with my fingers. After that, I pour water from the pitcher into the cup and rinse my mouth out properly. Wiping my face and mouth with the cloth, I think about how different this is than back home. It's not perfect, and it doesn't taste very good, but it works.

When I step out into the hallway, Aurelia is walking past me with a tray in her hands. She's heading toward Marcus's room, likely taking Lucius breakfast, which is a good sign. I hope he's well enough to eat because he'll need his strength to recover from his wounds.

"Aurelia," I say quietly. "I don't mean to bother you, but could I ask you a quick question?"

"Of course," she says, turning on her heel to face me.

"I don't remember going to bed last night. Do you know how I got there?"

"Dominus Valerius carried you," she says. "You fell asleep tending to his brother. He carried you to bed and then went back and slept in the chair beside Lucius."

"I see. Thank you," I reply, caught off guard.

She nods and continues past me, focused on her task.

I already knew Marcus was handsome—anyone can see that, with his dark eyes and hair, his chiseled bronze muscles, and a smile that could make any woman melt. But incredibly brave and kind enough to carry me to bed, too? That's going to be a problem for us. I need to convince him to help me get everyone out of this city within the next three days, and if I continue to develop romantic feelings for him, it could complicate everything.

I'm still thinking about Marcus and starting to consider how and when I'm going to tell him about Vesuvius when he comes out of the bedroom and walks down the hall. He stops when he sees me. His hair is mussed, and he has bags under his eyes, indicating he hasn't slept properly, but when he looks at me, he smiles.

"Good morning. Would you like to have breakfast with me?" he asks.

"Yes," I say, returning his smile.

We head toward the dining room together, and Felix follows us. At the table, Marcus pulls out my chair, but I hesitate before I lower myself into it.

"Actually," I say, "would it be all right if we brought our plates in from the kitchen? Aurelia's busy feeding Lucius his breakfast."

Marcus pauses and looks at me like he's considering my request. "You're absolutely right."

We turn and walk into the kitchen, Felix following in hopes of getting a scrap, no doubt.

The food is already plated on the hearth. A woman I haven't met moves between the counter and the fire. She looks up as we enter, clearly surprised to see us there instead of waiting in the dining room.

"Callista," Marcus says, "this is my friend, Fiona."

"It's very nice to meet you, Callista," I say. "You're an amazing cook."

"Thank you," she says softly. From her tone, and her wrinkled brow, it's obvious she's confused about why Marcus is in his own kitchen, and I find that a little amusing.

"We'll take our plates to the dining room," Marcus says, setting them on the tray. I pick up a couple of cups and a pitcher of water. We thank the cook, and she nods as we head back to the table.

When we return, we sit and serve ourselves. I feed a bite of my eggs to Felix and start eating, suddenly realizing how hungry I am.

"I wanted to thank you," Marcus says, "for last night. You stopped Lucius's chest wound from bleeding, which most likely saved his life. Thank you for following me, for going after Quintus, for coming back into that alley, and for staying with my brother. I've never met anyone like you, Fiona. You're the most courageous and selfless woman I've ever met."

For a moment, I'm speechless. He's such a good man, and it's the most genuine compliment I've received in a long time. I manage a simple, "You're welcome," but what I really want to say is that I'm drawn to him—that I'm from two thousand years in the future, and somehow, I think I was sent back in time to save his life.

"Fiona." He interrupts my thoughts once again, and I welcome the intrusion. "Would you like to join me in visiting Quintus at his home this morning, and then we can attend the parade?"

"Of course, I would love to. Are we bringing Quintus a thank you gift?"

He frowns. "A thank you gift?"

I tear off a piece of bread and hand it down to Felix before answering. "Yes. We could get a nice basket and fill it with items like wine, figs, fruit, bread, and cheese. Just something small to show we're grateful for what he did last night. Maybe some quail eggs and fresh fish if you have them."

Marcus looks at me for a moment, then nods, seeming a little surprised. "That's a very good idea. We'll do that."

I smile. "Good."

After breakfast, I follow Marcus back into the kitchen. "Callista," he says, "would you please help us put together a basket for Quintus and his family?"

Felix pads along with us as we fill the basket together. While we work on our little project, I still can't stop thinking about how I'm going to tell Marcus what I need to say, but for just a little while, it seems like everything isn't about to be buried in ash.

We leave his house together, with Felix trotting close at our heels. The streets are already busy with morning workers as we walk. Marcus carries the basket, and I follow his lead when we turn down the road toward Quintus's house.

When we arrive, Marcus knocks, and Quintus opens the door. "Good morning!"

"Good morning." Marcus smiles. "Quintus, you remember Fiona."

"I do," he says. "Good morning, Fiona."

"Good morning." I give a little wave.

We go inside, and Felix slips through before either of us can fully enter.

"Felix!" Julia and Gaius call out immediately, both of them running toward him. The girl drops to her knees and wraps her arms around his neck while Gaius pats his head, and Felix wags his tail with joy.

Cornelia comes in from the kitchen a moment later, wiping her hands on her apron, and her eyes move first to Marcus, then to me, and finally to the basket. "You brought a gift?" she asks.

"A small token of my gratitude for last night," Marcus answers.

Quintus shuts the door. "You didn't need to do that."

"It was Fiona's idea," Marcus says, "but honestly, I could never fully repay you."

Cornelia takes the basket, lifting the cloth and looking over the goodies inside. "Thank you so much," she says. "We can use all of this."

"You're welcome," Marcus says before turning to Quintus. "We're going to the forum. Will I see you there later?"

"Yes," Quintus replies. "We'll be there this afternoon."

Cornelia nods. "We'll see you there around sunset for the parade." She looks at me. "It was lovely seeing you again, Fiona."

"Likewise, Cornelia. Until this evening," I reply, following Marcus toward the door.

We all exchange goodbyes, Gaius still petting Felix while Julia gives him one last hug before we head out.

We step back into the street together, and Marcus whistles for Felix, who runs up behind us, while the morning noise of the city picks up around us. We make our way toward the forum.

A few blocks later, I get a rush of adrenaline, and I know I can't wait any longer. I have to warn Marcus about Vesuvius, even if I sound crazy. Even if he locks me up and throws away the key, I have to at least try to tell him. All over the city there are people like Quintus and his family. They're beautiful families with darling children, and I can't wait another moment.

"Marcus," I begin, taking a deep breath. "I have something to tell you, and it will sound absurd."

"You can tell me anything," he says, not for the first time, meeting my gaze.

I blurt it all out before I lose my nerve. "I'm not really from the north, Marcus. I'm not really even from this time. I was sent back in time from two thousand years in the future to warn you about something horrible that is going to happen to your city within the next three days."

Marcus stops walking and stares at me with his head tipped to the side, his eyebrows knit together.

"The day you saw me on the temple steps, I was going there to tell the priest of Venus my message. I was hoping he would warn the people, but he didn't believe me, and he called me a liar. I promise you I'm telling the truth."

"Fiona, did you hit your head? Did you not sleep well last night?" he asks.

"I'm well, and I slept fine. Please, just listen. I am from the year 2026. I was here, digging through the ruins of what used to be your city after a great natural disaster… and then I fell through time, and I ended up here. In three days, *everything* and *everyone* around us will be buried in ash and dust when Vesuvius erupts. The mountain will explode so quickly it will cover Pompeii entirely in ash."

His eyes stay on mine, searching my face as if something in it will give him an answer that makes sense of what he has just heard.

"I…." He stops, exhales, and continues. "I don't know what to say. I don't know whether I can believe such a story."

"I would never lie to you," I say. "I just want you to help me save as many people as we can."

Marcus looks around us to make sure no one is listening and escorts me off the main street into a narrow side alley between the buildings, where fewer people pass, and Felix joins us.

I lean against the wall of a building, suddenly feeling exhausted, undoubtedly from the weight of my confession. Marcus looks into my eyes again, and I find myself wishing once more that he wasn't so damn gorgeous because it makes everything feel even more difficult.

"Vesuvius… the mountain outside the city is going to erupt?" he asks.

I nod. "Yes, on the twenty-fourth of this month. In just a few days."

"And you are telling this to me because you thought I might be able to help get the people out of the city?"

"Together, I think we can make a difference and change history," I reply. "You have the power and the influence to save many lives, Marcus."

He steps closer, as though he is reading my eyes, trying to decide if I am a lunatic or a liar. I hold my breath, waiting for him to call me a liar. Instead, he asks quietly, "Where should we begin?"

And when he says that, I realize he believes me, and all the tension I've been carrying alone rises to the surface. All my feelings of fear, confusion, anxiety, and doubt unravel, and I step forward and kiss him. Our lips brush softly at first, and then his hands are on my waist, pulling me closer while deepening the kiss into something more passionate and meaningful. When we finally pull back, something has shifted between us. We are now partners in this misery, ready to see how many citizens of Pompeii we can rescue together.

16

WORD SPREADS

Fiona has just kissed me, and I can't help but smile, still reeling from the shock. A woman initiating a kiss… that alone should tell me she's telling the truth about being from another era.

"Tell me," I say finally, "what's our first course of action?"

At first I didn't believe her. A woman from the future? Vesuvius erupting in just a few days? It sounds preposterous, but why would she lie about being from the future or about Vesuvius covering the city in ash?

She is kind, selfless, and brave. She helped Lucius and me without hesitation and consistently helps my servants. She asks for nothing in return other than a roof over her head and a meal once in a while, and I have to admit, it begins to make a kind of sense that she's not from this time. Where else would she have come from that she can't simply find her way back?

"Is there a place we could move the festival—outside of the city, away from the mountain?" Fiona asks.

I think about her question for a moment and realize we can simultaneously move the festival and protect the people. "Yes, there is a way." I think it through quickly. "The meadow near the vineyards far northwest of town. It's far enough from Vesuvius and the city, but still accessible to the people."

"That's a brilliant idea," she says. "And you're the one with the authority to make that change."

"I don't have the authority on my own," I admit. "But I have a brief meeting with the council members already scheduled for this morning. I will convince them that it's for the best." I have no idea how I will do that, but money talks. I'll have to focus on that.

"Then, we'll have to tell all the vendors," she says, tapping her chin, lost in thought.

"We'll do it together," I say. "Come on. I don't want to be late."

Fiona and I make it to the council meeting just in time. She waits outside as she's not allowed in. Only members are. I wait patiently for my turn to talk. Some of the other members are concerned about the lack of sales at the forum. I use that to my advantage and suggest we move to where there's more room, where we can have more live entertainment.

The pushback is hard, especially at first. Of course, the festival has to happen in the forum, but the more I talk about a lack of revenue, the more they understand. Finally, the council agrees. We should move the festival. As soon as the meeting is over, I rush outside. "Fiona!" I say, finding her standing with Felix beneath a tree. "We did it!"

She squeals and wraps her arms around my neck. "You mean you did it!" She kisses my cheek, and my stomach twists into a knot. Her touch has my skin lighting on fire.

When we get to the forum, we'll start spreading the word. The last three days of the festival—August twenty-second through the twenty-fourth—will be moved to the open meadow past the vineyards."

We start at the edge of the forum with the first stall, Felix tagging along at my heel.

"Good morning," I say to a man selling fabric. "We are going to change the location of the festival for the last three days."

He looks at me like I've lost my mind. "Moving? Where?" he asks.

"To the meadow past the vineyards northwest of town," I say.

"There will be more space there, and people will come through to buy your wares."

Fiona adds, "There will also be more room for performances, which will draw a larger crowd. You'll reach more people than you do here. And please, tell the other vendors, and all of your customers."

He studies us for a moment but then nods and goes back to his work. I see him shaking his head in confusion, probably thinking about how difficult it will be for him to move everything. He'll thank me later.

We move on to a woman selling sandals. "The festival is moving for the last three days," Fiona says.

"Why would you move it out of the forum?" she asks.

"It has outgrown this space," I say. "The meadow northwest of the city will hold more stalls, more people and make room for more activity. The council just made the decision."

Fiona says, "You won't lose business. You will *gain* it. People will have more room to shop."

"Please share the message with everyone you meet today," I add.

The woman ponders our announcement. "Dominus, this is your funeral," she says with a grin and a wink.

If only she knew. I smile back at her, and we keep moving, Felix staying close. We stop near an open space where a group of dancers are gathered together, stretching and practicing their routine.

"Good morning," I say. "I have an important announcement. The last three days of the festival are being moved."

They all exchange shocked looks. "Moved where?" the tall, lanky one asks.

"To the meadow past the vineyards far northwest of town," I say. "There will be more people coming through."

Fiona adds, "And more space for performances. You will have a larger audience than you would here."

They pause, taking that in.

"It's by order of the council. And please tell the others," I say. "Anyone performing in the festival. The location changes are for August twenty-second through the twenty-fourth."

They nod. "We will tell them."

We keep moving, Felix staying close at my side as we walk into the bakery. He lets out a soft whine, and I glance down as his ears perk forward.

"All right," I murmur.

I step up and buy him a fresh loaf, still warm. When I turn back, Felix is already watching me like he knows exactly what he's getting. I tear off a piece and feed it to him. He takes it eagerly, and then I turn back to the baker.

"The festival is moving for the last three days," I tell him.

"Is something wrong?" he asks.

"No," Fiona says. "It is being expanded."

"Expanded?"

"Yes," I say. "More space. More people. We'll provide stalls for those of you who have your own shops. Just bring your baked goods, and we'll have a place all set up for you." I've already cleared this with the council.

"Thank you, Dominus," he says, returning to his work.

We step back out into the forum as Felix finishes chewing, and I give him another bite. He follows as we move, eating as he goes.

The temple is just ahead, its courtyard already busy with people gathering. As Fiona and I pass through, we spread the message again and again—relaying that the festival is moving to a larger space, and there will be more room for performances, a larger audience, and more business for the stalls and traders. By the time we reach the far side of the forum again, the word is already spreading.

As we walk, I start to worry about how I'm going to tell Quintus about Vesuvius and the change in the festival venue. Everything has become complicated so quickly, and I'm not sure how to manage each step of this journey. Fortunately, I have someone with me who always seems to know exactly what to do and say in every situation.

I look over at Fiona. "I'm struggling with how to tell Quintus," I admit. "After all of our work—days and days of planning and preparing for the festival—it's been decided at the last minute to uproot the entire celebration and change the location. He will be confused at the least, if not angry at me."

Fiona reaches for my hand. "Let's talk it over, but I think we should get a drink of water first."

"That's a good idea," I say, happily holding her hand in mine as we walk. "And Felix could use some water, too."

We drink from the fountain, and I make sure Felix gets some water as well before we find a shady spot and sit down.

"Do you think Quintus will believe us if we tell him Vesuvius is going to erupt?" she asks, glancing back toward the forum. "We shouldn't be telling everyone the truth. We don't want people to panic. There would be chaos in the streets." She looks up at me. "But what do you think about telling Quintus and Cornelia the truth?"

"I think that's a good idea," I say. "I just wasn't sure you'd agree. I don't know how they're going to react, but if anyone is going to listen, it's them."

We spend the rest of the morning moving through the forum and the nearby streets, delivering our message over and over.

At midday, we stop long enough to eat lunch in the shade. We get bread, olives, cheese, and grilled pork from a street stall. Felix gets more than his fair share of the pork.

The afternoon is more of the same. We walk, we talk, we repeat the message until it feels like we've been everywhere twice. Eventually, most people already seem to know it before we reach them. Word spreads faster than we can keep up with, and I believe an official decree from the council has also been made.

By the time the sun starts to set, we meet Quintus and his family at the location where the parade will launch. Torches are being lit, and priests and priestesses are getting in line, as well as the other performers and participants.

"Good evening, Quintus," I say, walking up to them. "Could I have a moment with you and Cornelia? Privately, please?"

Fiona looks at Cornelia. "Would it be all right if I take Gaius, Julia, and Felix up to the grassy area to play for a bit? Just so you three can speak in peace."

Cornelia studies her for a moment and then nods. "Yes, that would be fine."

Fiona inclines her head in thanks before leading the children away toward the grassy rise above the forum, Felix bounding up the hill behind them.

Once they are out of earshot, Quintus and Cornelia turn back to me. I lower my voice. "The council has changed the festival location, in case you haven't heard. The last three days will be held in the meadow past the vineyards well northwest of the town."

"They've already moved forward with this? After all the work we've put into this festival?" Quintus asks, his tone a mixture of shock and confusion.

"There are things happening with the mountain," I say quietly. "We're trying to get everyone out of the city and away from Vesuvius. Staying here is no longer something we can risk."

Quintus's eyes narrow. "What are you talking about? And how do you know this?"

Cornelia looks at me for a moment, her eyebrows arched. "Marcus, you're scaring me."

I keep my voice quiet. "There's no reason to be afraid because we know about it ahead of time, and you will be far enough away that it won't hurt you or your children, but friends, Vesuvius is going to erupt."

Quintus's jaw drops. "And how could you know such a thing?"

"Explain yourself properly, Marcus," Cornelia adds.

"I wouldn't have asked for this change unless I was certain enough to act on it, and I need you to trust me. On the twenty-fourth of August, Vesuvius is going to erupt and cover the city in ash. Whether you help us relocate the festival or not, I just need you to be safe— take everything you can carry and leave the city," I explain.

Cornelia's eyes search my face. "You're serious?"

Quintus doesn't look away from me. "Marcus doesn't lie. I trust him with my life." He turns to Cornelia. "We will help relocate the festival, take our children, and leave."

Relief hits me. "Thank you for trusting me. Take your valuables, anything sentimental, and go. Start over somewhere new... and be grateful you lived to tell the tale."

"Where should we move to?" Cornelia asks, her gaze moving from Quintus to me and back to her husband.

"I'll go with Fiona and my family to Neapolis," I say.

Quintus gives a single nod. "Neapolis it is."

"Good, then it's settled," I say, clapping Quintus on the shoulder.

I look back toward Fiona and the children playing and lift my hand. "Fiona," I call, waving them back over.

Just before the parade begins, Fiona comes back with Julia, Gaius, and Felix, and we watch the procession move through the forum. Dancers in bright colored outfits lead the way and are followed by jugglers tossing their props in the air above the moving line of performers.

Behind them come musicians playing flutes and drums, the sound carrying across the open space as the procession continues through the streets lined with spectators. The priests and priestesses at the end of the line, moving with formal precision, carry the symbols of the gods as the parade advances around the square.

I look over at Fiona and know that she is the hero in all of this. She's the one who will save them all, and I will do whatever it takes to help.

17

ELECTRICITY

FIONA

I watch the children's faces light up as the parade moves through the square. Julia points toward the dancers. "Can I be like them when I'm big, Mother?"

"Of course you can, if that's what you want, sweetheart," Cornelia says.

Gaius catches a ball one of the jugglers tosses his way and immediately hands it to Felix. The dog lies down and chews on it, making the children burst into giggles.

I look up at Marcus and am completely amazed by him. He could've laughed in my face when I told him I'm from the future. He could've called me a liar and a lunatic when I told him that the mountain is going to erupt… but he didn't. He trusts me, and he believes me enough to help me get the people of Pompeii to safety. We might just change history within the next couple of days, all the while being drawn to one another in a way that is causing me to want to lean over and kiss him again right this second. It wouldn't be good etiquette, so I control myself, though I find myself yearning to be alone with him.

"Did you tell them?" I whisper in his ear.

"I did. They trust us. Quintus said he'll help relocate the festival, and then he's taking his family to Neapolis."

I smile up at him. "I'm so glad."

"Yes, tomorrow we'll go to my parents' house and convince them that they're going to have to move. I don't know how we'll do that. They've lived in the same house for thirty-five years."

"We'll figure it out," I say. "I'll help you."

He nods. "It's been a long day. Would you like to retire? We could go check on Lucius and then perhaps have a drink?"

"That sounds wonderful right now." I squeeze his hand, thankful to have met such an amazing man.

Marcus leans over to tell Quintus that we're leaving, but I can't hear Quintus's reply over the parade drums, though I assume he's telling Marcus when and where they'll meet again. When they're done, we wave goodbye to Cornelia and the children, and Marcus whistles for Felix as we walk away. The dog jumps up and follows us, parts of the stuffed ball in his mouth, other parts littering the street.

We walk back to Marcus's neighborhood under the light of the moon. "I'm sorry I'm not very talkative tonight. We used our voices quite a bit today," he says.

I turn to him. "It's thoughtful of you to apologize, but it's not necessary. I understand completely."

He reaches over, takes my hand, and a jolt of electricity runs through me. I hope I'm not blushing too much, but our kiss earlier was incredible, and I hope we get the chance to do it again soon.

When we reach his house, he unlocks the door and holds it open. Felix and I step inside first, and the dog goes straight to his food and water as if he hasn't eaten all day.

"You must be starving, Felix," Marcus jokes.

"Yes, I hear his owner is a cruel man who serves him nothing but gruel," I tease.

Marcus laughs as he closes the door and locks it behind us. "I think I'll go give the staff the night off. Make yourself at home, and I'll return in just a moment."

I nod, intrigued by the idea of Marcus dismissing his servants, and make myself comfortable on his sofa while I wait. My feet are killing me—we've been walking all day.

When he returns, Marcus asks, "Would you like to come with me to my bedroom and check on Lucius?"

"Yes," I say quietly. "Perhaps I can be of some help to him."

As we walk down the hall, Marcus whispers, "He might be asleep. Aurelia said he was feeling much better—that he was talking and ate well today—but that he is still in a lot of pain and needs to rest."

I nod. "I'll be quiet," I reply.

We get to the door of his room, and Marcus lightly knocks. When Lucius doesn't answer, he slowly opens the door and steps inside. I watch him from the threshold as he checks on his brother, feeling his forehead, checking for fever, and leaning down to make sure he is breathing normally.

When Marcus is satisfied, he comes back to the door, and I step out into the hallway with him. He softly closes the door behind him.

"I think he's going to be all right," he whispers.

I nod, and we both walk back into the living room.

"He will definitely recover, thanks to you," I say. "You saved his life. But how are we going to get Lucius out of the city?"

"You bring up a good point," he says, stepping over to where his wine is kept, choosing a bottle and a couple of goblets. "He'll definitely need to use my carriage. In fact, I should send him ahead tomorrow." We sit down together on his sofa, each with a goblet of wine in hand, and Marcus looks at me. "You're very brave," he says quietly, resting his hand on my knee. "To tell me… to trust me with your secret. Not many people could do what you did, and I feel very grateful to be able to know you."

I shake my head, feeling a flush creep up my neck. "I had to," I whisper. "If no one knew…"

"And you're thoughtful and kind," he interjects. "You're trying to make sure as many people survive as possible. I've never met anyone like you. Will you tell me more—about your time?"

I pause, thinking about how to say it without sounding foolish or overwhelming him. "In my time, cities are enormous. Buildings rise so high you almost can't see the top from the ground. People live stacked above one another in levels all the way up. We don't travel with horses," I continue. "We have vehicles that move on their own. They're like carriages but with engines that move faster than any animal. You could get to Neapolis in half an hour."

He gasps. "Surely, you're not serious?"

I laugh. "I'm completely serious."

"Moving that quickly must be phenomenal. Please tell me more."

I feel the wine going to my head and the warmth of Marcus's hand on my knee. Smiling, I continue to tell him about the future. "Like some of your buildings here, clean water runs into every home through pipes in the walls. No one has to carry it or fetch it. It just runs straight into the tub or the sink. And light isn't from a flame. We make it from something called electricity. It runs through wires, and you can turn on a light whenever you need it."

Marcus looks at me for a moment, trying to imagine it. "So everyday life is much easier?"

"So much easier. And people live longer. There are places called hospitals where sick and injured people go to become well. Illnesses that would kill people in your time are easily treated in mine."

"You must miss your own time," he says, his tone more serious now.

"I do, but I'm finding this place to be more enjoyable every day. There's something else you should know," I say, placing my empty goblet on the table in front of us. Marcus sets his down, too. "In my time, women are much more direct about what they want. And, Marcus... I want you." I feel bold and brave at the moment, looking at him this way, knowing all that is about to happen.

He stares at me for a moment before he leans in and kisses me gently. Message received.

I wrap my hand around his bicep as his mouth opens to mine, deepening the kiss. He moves his hands to my waist, pulling me closer. The kiss intensifies—hungry and urgent–until I shift my body to straddle his lap on the sofa.

His hands roam up my back, finding the clasp of my stola. He unpins it with a flick, and the fabric loosens, slipping down my shoulders to expose my breasts. I moan into his mouth as he cups my bare skin, thumbs circling my hardening nipples.

I tug at the ties of his tunic, loosening the fabric until it falls open, revealing his smooth, tan, toned chest. I rake my nails over his pecs, feeling his muscles tense beneath my touch.

He pulls back from our kiss, just long enough to take off his tunic completely, his cock already straining against the undergarment wrapped around his hips. I reach down, untying the knot, freeing his thick shaft.

I wrap my hand around him. Marcus groans, his hands sliding down to hike up the hem of my under-tunic. He pushes it aside, exposing me, already wet and aching for him. His fingers part my folds, and I gasp, rocking against his hand.

"Fiona, you're so beautiful," he says, his voice rough as he finds my most sensitive spot.

I can't help myself. The sofa creaks under us as I lift my hips again, positioning him at my entrance. I sink down slowly, inch by inch. A whimper escapes my lips as I take him fully, clenching around his length. Marcus's hands grip my bottom, guiding me as I ride him.

His hips buck up to meet mine with each thrust. I brace my hands on his shoulders, nails digging in, as the pleasure builds. He captures my breast in his mouth, teeth grazing the sensitive peak, and I cry out, grinding down harder.

He moves inside me, close to the edge, and I clench my inner walls around him. The sensation tips me over the precipice, waves of ecstasy crashing through me. I shudder on top of him and feel his warmth spread inside of me. We're both spent, collapsing together on the sofa in a tangle of limbs and discarded clothes.

"That was amazing," he whispers, kissing my cheek. "You're incredible, Fiona."

Looking into his eyes, I say, "I'm so glad I found you, Marcus." I rest my head on his cheek, feeling secure in a world that's falling apart because his arms are around me.

As we lie here together, I think about the last few days. When I got on the plane to Italy, I never imagined myself in ancient Pompeii, and I certainly never imagined falling in love with a man of this era. Now, as Marcus holds me close, I have no doubt that I belong with him.

1 8

PLANS

MARCUS

Fiona lies next to me on the sofa, moonlight streaming in the window next to us, and I still feel the echoes of what we just shared. I think of her curves pressed against me and the way I lost myself in her gorgeous eyes through every moan and gasp.

She's beautiful, yes, but there's more to her than that. Being with her, feeling her body against mine, it was more than desire. I realize we haven't known each other long, but it's true. I'm in love with her.

I press a kiss to her forehead. "Would you like to go to bed?" I ask, my voice low.

She nods, a tired, satisfied smile on her lips. "Yes."

We pull on our tunic and stola, and I lead her to the guest bedroom. Once we're under the covers, she leans into me, and I wrap an arm around her. I keep thinking about how impossible this should be. She's from two thousand years in the future, and yet, the pull between us is so strong that she found me. She saved me. And now, together, we're going to save my city. She has to have been sent by the gods.

"Rest well, Fiona," I whisper into her ear.

"You too, Marcus. Goodnight," she whispers back.

I've always wanted a wife, someone I could protect and love. I didn't know if that would ever happen for me, but as we fall asleep with our arms around each other, I let my mind drift to dreams of a life with Fiona.

I WAKE TO FIND FIONA BESIDE ME, HALF ASLEEP, MORNING LIGHT illuminating her golden hair.

"Good morning." I nuzzle her gently.

"Good morning." She stretches and yawns.

"So," I say, climbing from bed and locating a fresh tunic, "today we'll need to get Lucius out of the city."

She nods, fixing her stola. I wish I had another to offer her, but I don't. "And then we must convince your parents to leave the city as well. All while moving the festival to a different location."

I grin. "It sounds like a long day. Breakfast first?"

"Definitely breakfast first." She grins at me, running her fingers through her hair to untangle it.

We finish getting dressed and washing up for the day. Fiona braids her hair, and then we head toward the kitchen.

On the way to the dining room, we pass Felix. He lifts his head, rises, and follows us. When we reach the table, Aurelia is already there, setting out our plates and filling our cups.

"Thank you, Aurelia," I say, nodding. "How is Lucius today?"

"He's feeling much better," she replies with a hopeful nod.

"Is he well enough to travel by carriage?" I pull Fiona's chair out and then sit beside her.

Aurelia tilts her head thoughtfully. "I believe he could manage it."

"Very well," I say. "Please get him ready to travel. I am sending him to Neapolis."

"Of course, Dominus," Aurelia says. "I'll see to it immediately."

"Thank you, Aurelia," I say as she bows and leaves the room.

Fiona and I dig into our breakfast, and Felix eats from his bowl on the floor in the corner.

"Are you going to tell Lucius the truth about why you're sending him to Neapolis?" Fiona asks.

"No." I shrug and take another bite.

"How will you convince him to go?"

"I'll send him with enough money to buy a house," I reply. "And I'll send my belongings so he can furnish the place he chooses. I'll tell him to lie low in Neapolis for a while and hide from the people he is indebted to."

She nods. "Wonderful idea, Marcus."

"Thank you. I just hope it works."

After breakfast, Fiona follows me outside, Felix at my heel. "Where are we going?" she asks.

"I need to speak with Titus," I tell her. I call for him, and he approaches, his head bowed.

"I need two carriages prepared," I say. "One for Lucius and the servants and one for my belongings. Everything of value that can be carried from the house will go. The servants will travel with Lucius to Neapolis. You will take him there and see that he is settled. I will give him the money to buy a house, and you will make sure it is furnished with my belongings and livable while he recovers. I want everything and everyone ready to leave tomorrow morning."

Titus hesitates, clearly confused, but he keeps his tone calm. "It will be done, Dominus."

"Titus," I say, softer now. "I promise, in a few days this will all make sense. Just trust me."

He nods once and walks away.

Fiona watches him go. "Well," she says, glancing sideways at me, "that went well."

I laugh. "It could've gone worse." I take a deep breath, reminding myself that most of my servants do not have families here, and those that do will be able to take them with them. "Now, would you like to meet my mother and father?"

"I don't think I have a choice," she jests, still smiling.

We walk toward my parents' house, Felix running ahead, chasing after a bird along the road.

"Are we going to tell your parents about Vesuvius?" Fiona asks.

I shake my head. "No. I don't think they'll believe us. They will think I've lost my mind."

"Then how will we get them to leave their home?"

"We'll have to find another reason. Something they'll accept without question."

Fiona nods. "How many carriages do they have?"

"They have three. One they use and two in the carriage house. Why? What is that brilliant mind of yours thinking?" I ask with a wink.

She shares her idea with me, and by the time we reach my childhood home, we have a plan to get my mother and father to Neapolis and safety. I am nearly confident it will work.

Before we go inside, I stop in the front garden and look at Fiona. "So all of this is going to be covered in ash?" I ask. "None of it will survive?"

"When Vesuvius erupts, it unleashes ash, heat, and debris," she says. "Entire buildings will collapse under it. Some houses, shops and walls are buried and preserved, but most of what's exposed is destroyed. And people... they're buried where they fall. That's why your city is one of the most important places for archaeologists like me—people who study history from the Earth itself—to dig. We have been able to make plaster molds in the places where the bodies lay for so long. Mothers' bodies bracing over their children—families reaching out to one another—so hauntingly sad, Marcus. Their lives are preserved so we can learn from them."

Her description rolls over me in waves of grief and pain. I wipe a tear from the corner of my eye and take a deep breath to calm my nerves before speaking with my parents.

Fiona seems to see that I'm struggling and reaches over to squeeze my hand. "We will save them. As many as we can," she whispers. "Let's make sure your family is safe first."

I nod. "You're right." I open the door, and we step inside the foyer.

Lydia greets us immediately. "Good morning, Dominus," she says. "I'll fetch your parents."

"Thank you, Lydia." I escort Fiona into the sitting room while Felix lies down near the front door. We sit on the sofa together. I try not to let my nervous energy turn into a fidget. A moment later, footsteps echo in the hall, and my parents enter.

"Marcus," my mother says, crossing the room to wrap me in a warm embrace.

My father sits in the chair across from us. "It's good to see you, son."

"It's wonderful to see you both. This is my very good friend, Fiona." I gesture to where she stands nearby.

My mother smiles at her. "It's a pleasure to meet you, Fiona."

She nods. "It's a pleasure to meet you as well."

"Welcome," Father says with a smile.

"Thank you," Fiona says. "You have a beautiful home."

"Thank you," my mother says. "To what do we owe the pleasure of your visit?"

I take a deep breath, bracing myself for their reactions. "Mother, Father, I have something very sad to tell you."

Mother leans forward, worry written in every wrinkle on her face. "Whatever it is, son, I'm certain everything will be all right."

Father's voice is rough, tight with anxiety. "Well, just tell us, Marcus. Don't make us wait."

"Lucius was beaten again," I say. "Fiona and I were able to save him, but his injuries were far worse than before. He nearly died."

Mother clutches her hands to her chest, and her face turns pale.

"What… what are we going to do with that boy?" Father asks.

"I'm sending him to Neapolis," I tell them. "He'll have plenty of money and furnishings to set up a home. It's the only way he can get away from those he owes debts to. He needs safety and distance. I need you to go to Neapolis, too," I continue. "Take your furniture, your valuables, anything sentimental, and your servants—everything you'd want long-term. I need you to stay there and live near Lucius. You have to make sure he's safe, support him, and keep him from harm. Fiona and I will join you within the week."

Father looks at me, then Mother, and then back at me. "Surely, you're not serious?" he asks.

"Marcus, we're old. We've lived in this house our entire marriage. We can't just leave," my mother adds.

I hate to strike at their hearts, and I hate to make them feel guilty, but I know it's the only way to save their lives. Fiona said the people here will all die—that they'll pass away holding the ones they love—and I just can't let that happen to my mother and father.

"Would you rather keep your house… or your son?" I ask bluntly.

Mother's hands fly to her mouth. Her eyes glisten, but she swallows and nods. "We'll go, Marcus. We'll leave… for now. We can always come back later, when it's safe for Lucius, too."

Father gives me a nod. "Yes. You're right. We'll go. Whatever it takes to keep Lucius safe."

"We'll start making plans to leave," Mother says.

"I need you to be ready to leave by tomorrow morning," I say.

"Tomorrow morning? That's far too soon. We can't even pack that quickly," Father protests.

Fiona speaks up cautiously. "If I may interject… Lucius said he didn't want to go either. He needs to leave, and if you're ready and leaving at the same time as him, he'll be more willing to go."

After a moment, Father sighs. "All right. Tomorrow morning it is. We'll make it work."

"Well," Mother adds, "at least we'll have all of our servants with us. And my cousins, Antonio and Aemilia, live in Neapolis—it will be good to see them. We can always come back as soon as we like. It's not that far away."

"Yes, Mother." My heart breaks at having to bend the truth to keep them safe. "It will all be worth it." I take a step toward the door. "Fiona and I have things to attend to at the festival today, so we can't stay, but just remember to take everything you'll need. Pack your clothes, furnishings, anything sentimental that you care about—and meet me at my house at dawn tomorrow with all three carriages full."

Mother and Father walk us to the door, and I hug them each goodbye.

"It was lovely to meet you," Fiona says as we step outside.

"Lovely to meet you as well," Mother replies. She disappears back inside the house, probably to begin packing.

Father pats Felix on the head before my dog joins Fiona and me in the front garden. I watch as he closes the door, and then we step out into the street.

As we walk, Fiona looks at me. "Did you think that would work? That your parents would go along with it so easily, or did you expect them to be more stubborn?"

I shake my head. "I hated putting them in that position, and using guilt to guide them, but I'm relieved they agreed. They'll be safe, and that's what matters."

"You're right. You did the right thing. Are you ready to move an entire festival?" She smiles and takes my hand.

I laugh. "As ready as I'll ever be."

The sun has climbed higher, and the day will be over before we know it. Now that we have a plan to save my family and our servants, an entire city still needs rescuing. It sounds intimidating, but if anyone can pull it off, it's the incredibly beautiful, fair-haired goddess by my side.

19

FALLING

FIONA

We spent all afternoon moving the festival from the forum to the meadow northwest of the city. My arms ache from hauling crates, draping banners, and helping set up booths. Marcus, Quintus, Cornelia, even little Julia and Gaius, are finally catching their breath. Felix lies in the grass between the children. He's exhausted, too.

The meadow is alive with activity. Vendors set up their stalls, traders arrange their goods, dancers rehearse, and musicians tune their instruments. The priests and priestesses move among the crowd, praying over people and welcoming everyone to the new location for the celebration.

When we take a moment to rest in the shade, Cornelia glances at Marcus, then back at me. "Not to be overly critical, but may I ask why you chose this spot? The route here took us closer to the mountain at first. You're certain this is the right direction?"

I glance toward the peak, already casting a dark silhouette in the late afternoon light. "We chose this place because it's on the way to Neapolis," I say. "People will need to start leaving the area the night before or the morning of the eruption."

"Yes," Marcus adds. "We'll be able to manage the crowd better here. Tomorrow night after the last performance, we'll announce that everyone can stay the night—but that Vesuvius will erupt the next day at noon, and they must leave the city."

Cornelia nods. "Yes, that makes sense. You've planned this carefully."

Quintus steps closer. "We've already packed the carriage and everything we'll need. We plan to leave at sunset, before the roads get crowded. I've brought plenty of torches to keep the road lit so the horses will be able to see."

"Perfect," Marcus says, reaching into his pouch and handing Quintus a handful of coins. "Take these. You're a great friend and assistant. We'll meet up with you in Neapolis."

Quintus bows his head. "Thank you, Marcus. This will make everything much easier."

Cornelia smiles. "Yes, we're grateful. Truly."

I look up at Marcus, and my affection for him grows. Even in the middle of all this chaos, he's thinking of others.

He claps Quintus on the shoulder. "Should we get everyone something to eat?"

Quintus nods. "Yes, that sounds good."

Marcus glances at me. "We'll be back in a bit."

I nod, and the men walk away to choose us something for dinner. Felix lifts his head, his tail thumping on the ground, but he's so tired that he doesn't even follow Marcus.

"Fiona," Cornelia says. "I know you just met, but have you thought about marrying Marcus? Starting a family? It's obvious he's crazy about you."

Shocked by her bold question, I'm momentarily at a loss for words. When I finally gather my thoughts, I reply, "I'm not sure what tomorrow or the next day holds for Marcus and me. Right now, we're just focused on getting everyone out of here alive."

Cornelia nods. "Yes, you're right. I was just thinking of something a little lighter than ash falling from the sky." She takes my hand. "And I would love to be here for you in your journey with Marcus when the time is right. If you need anything—from advice from an old married woman to how to bake a loaf of bread or how to raise a fussy baby—I'm here for you."

"I can't tell you how much that means to me, Cornelia. Thank you."

I consider what it means to have a friend here, in a time and place so far from anything I've ever known. I'm two thousand years in the past, with no one who fully understands me, and yet, here she is—offering guidance, sharing life, and treating me like I belong.

Marcus and Quintus return, each carrying a basket and a jug. Marcus sets his down. "I've got bread, cheese, and fruit. There's plenty for everyone."

"And here's smoked fish, olives, and more water." Quintus positions his between us and the children.

Cornelia hands Julia a piece of bread. "Here you go, little one."

"Thank you, Momma," Julia says, munching on the bread.

Crouching next to Gaius, the mother pours some water from the jug into their canteen. "Both of you drink plenty of water." Gaius takes a sip, and Cornelia hands him a slice of bread and a hunk of cheese.

I take a little of everything, looking over at Marcus. "Thank you."

He smiles. "We all need to eat. We've been working too hard." He breaks off a piece of fish and holds it out to Felix, who swallows it in one bite.

As I look at Quintus's beautiful family, I think about time, fate, and destiny. I was able to warn them, and now they will survive one of the most brutal natural disasters of all time. How could anyone deny the miracle in that?

When we finish our meal, Quintus stands. "It's getting late. We should get on the road."

Cornelia nods, and he helps her to her feet. "Everything's packed. The carriage is ready. The children will most likely sleep the whole way to our new home."

Marcus steps forward. "We'll see you in Neapolis. Take care on the road."

Quintus bows. "We will. Thank you—for everything."

Cornelia meets my eyes. "Yes, thank you. You've saved us all."

I stand and squeeze both her hands. "Be careful. I'll see you again soon."

The children wave enthusiastically, jumping up and down. "Bye!"

Marcus and I hug each of them, and then they hug Felix, stroking his fur before Quintus lifts both children into his arms. Together, they head toward their carriage.

"I don't know what we'd have done without you," Marcus says.

"Let's not think about that." I wipe a tear from my eye. "Let's go watch the dancers instead."

We walk to the stage, Felix following Marcus. The musicians play, and the dancers leap, dip, and twirl. We sit in front of the stage, and as I watch the show, my mind keeps drifting to the villages closer to Vesuvius. There's Herculaneum, Stabiae, Oplontis... and the tiny villas scattered through the countryside. Some residents will be buried by ash. Others will be killed by heat before anyone can escape. Saving Pompeii alone isn't enough.

Marcus shifts beside me, his eyes catching mine. "Fiona... what is it? You look upset."

I shake my head. "I was just thinking about how Pompeii isn't the only place in danger. The towns along the coast, the ones closer to the mountain—the people won't get out in time unless they're here when we give the warning."

He frowns. "How can we warn them, too? Tell me exactly what you're thinking."

"The festival," I say. "We used it to gather people safely here. We could do the same for the neighboring towns. I know they are each having their own festivals right now. We could invite them to join us in one large festival—framed as a celebration, performances, markets —they'd come for the festival and find safety outside the city walls."

Marcus nods. "We have one more full day. We'd need trusted messengers, the quickest routes mapped, and people to deliver the message without raising suspicion."

"Some invitations may need to be delivered in person by you," I add. "Officials will listen to other officials. I can go with you if you want. I know it's dangerous, but I can't stay silent when there are more people to save."

"We'll start tomorrow morning, after we send my family on their way," he says.

"That should work. Thank you, Marcus," I reply.

"Why are you thanking me? You're the hero here, Fiona." His gorgeous brown eyes catch the last light of day.

We watch the last of the dancing and juggling together. After the fire jugglers, Marcus buys some wine for us and a few pieces of fish that we share with Felix.

Marcus has encouraged most of the people to camp out here for the festival since we are so far away from Pompeii, but we must return to make sure his family and others are leaving the city, so we take a carriage the long distance back to his house. As we ride, the wine makes his hands wander—and so do mine.

When we reach his house, he closes the door behind us and takes my hand, leading me down the hall. The house is mostly empty and silent; Lucius and the servants are probably asleep, since they have to leave at dawn. Felix lies down in the hallway outside the guest room, just as he did last night.

Once Marcus closes the door, he pulls me into his arms right away. His hands slide around my waist, warm through my thin stola, and our lips meet softly at first, then deeper, as I press myself against his chest. He tastes like the wine we had earlier, and he moves me toward the bed without breaking us apart, his fingers trailing down my back.

I tug at his clothes, feeling the heat of his skin underneath. He shrugs his tunic off, letting it fall to the floor, and I run my hands over his chest, tracing the lines of his muscles.

He guides me down onto the mattress, his body covering mine. He kisses my neck, making me shiver as his hand slips under my stola, cupping my breast. I moan at his touch, my nipples hardening under his fingers as he circles them lightly.

I reach for his undergarments, pushing them down, and he's already hard and ready. He groans against my skin, his hips bucking as I stroke him.

He pulls my clothes off next, and then we're both entirely bare. His mouth finds my breast while his fingers tease between my thighs. I'm already wet, longing for him to send me over the edge.

"I need you, Fiona," he murmurs, positioning himself at my entrance. I wrap my legs around him, and he slides into me slowly, filling me up completely. We both sigh at the connection, his thrusts starting gently, building a steady rhythm.

I cling to his shoulders, matching his pace, our bodies moving together in the dim light of the bedroom. The pleasure builds perfectly until I feel the wave cresting. He kisses me deeply as I come undone, squeezing around his cock, and he follows soon after with a low moan.

We lie together, bodies still tangled, listening to each other's breathing.

"You are so beautiful," he says.

"You mean everything to me." I look into his eyes and can tell he's completely spent and about to fall asleep.

The last words that tumble from his lips before he closes his eyes are, "And I think I'm falling in love with you."

His breathing evens out, and I know he's asleep. A smile spreads across my face. I shouldn't be smiling. I should be terrified. We've only known each other a few days, and I'm from another century! I don't know if I can get home—or if I even *want* to. Vesuvius will erupt in less than forty-eight hours. We have to save the people. What right do we have to fall for each other in the middle of all this?! And yet... I am falling in love with him, too.

20

MIRACLE

MARCUS

I wake just before dawn to the sound of servants moving around the house, making final preparations for the long journey ahead. "Wake up," I whisper to Fiona as I get out of bed to dress, wash my face, and brush my teeth. She stretches, sits on the edge of the bed to re-braid her hair with just a sheet covering her beautiful body, and then rises and dresses for the day.

"Good morning." I can't help but chuckle as she looks like she's still half asleep.

She answers me with a soft, sleep-heavy, "Morning." Rising, she teeters across the floor and brushes her teeth. After she washes her face, I open the bedroom door to find the house is already alive. Felix is lying right outside the door, and he lifts his head but falls back asleep before we even step over him.

Fiona and I start down the hall together, and I notice the house seems different this morning. It doesn't feel like a home waking up but like something being emptied out. It's bittersweet. On one hand, it's a miracle that my servants and family will be saved, but on the other, it's sad to see my home so empty and know it's about to be buried in ash.

Aurelia is in the dining room, folding the last of the linens and placing them in a basket. "This is everything except the spare bedroom. It's all packed," she says. "Everything you requested is in the carriage, Dominus. Nothing was left behind."

I nod. "Thank you, Aurelia. And as I told Titus, in a few days, this will all make sense."

She smiles. "I trust you, Dominus. We'll get the guest room loaded up soon."

Titus appears in the doorway. "The carriages are ready," he says. "They're waiting outside. We'll load up the guest room contents and can leave as soon as you give the word."

"Thank you, Titus. I need to go tell my brother it's time to go," I say. Then I turn to Fiona. "I should have this conversation with Lucius alone."

She nods. "Of course."

I walk into my bedroom and find Lucius asleep in my bed, which will also still need to be loaded, but the rest of the room is empty. His face is pale in the dim light, his breathing uneven, like sleep is the only thing holding back the pain.

"Lucius?" I say quietly.

His eyes open slowly. It takes him a moment to find me.

"I need you to wake up. You're leaving for Neapolis," I tell him.

That wakes him fully. "What are you talking about, Marcus? Have you lost your mind? I told you, I don't want to go," he says, voice rough.

"I've already had everything prepared," I say. "The carriages are ready. You *are* going."

He shifts slightly, wincing as he tries to sit up. "I am not going anywhere."

"You are," I say. "It is safer there. You will recover properly."

"You are not my master, Marcus!"

"I have made the arrangements," I say bluntly. "Mother and Father will go with you. It is all settled. I'm giving you enough money to buy a house, and the carriages are packed with all of my furnishings and belongings. Mother and Father have packed all of your things into their carriage."

His eyes sharpen, anger cutting through the pain. "So this is decided for me?"

"Yes," I say. "And it's happening now. You gave up your liberty when you decided to put the entire family in danger, and when you almost got yourself killed. Twice."

"Very well," he mutters.

I help Lucius sit up, keeping hold of him until he's balanced. He's still too weak to move easily. I hand him his clothes from the foot of the bed and wait while he gets dressed. It's slow going. He's still stiff from the beating, and I help when he needs it, fixing things into place so he can dress without struggling.

When he's ready, I get him to his feet and keep an arm under him so he doesn't fall. We leave the room together, and I guide him through the house, moving slowly down the hall. When we walk past the dining room, Fiona comes over to help, and Lucius shifts his weight between her and me to make it easier for him to walk.

We make it through the front door and over to where the carriages are waiting. As I help him into one, he asks, "How did you get Mother and Father to agree to this?"

"Don't worry about it," I say, helping him inside and pressing the money into his hand. "Take this and buy a nice house. Fiona and I will join you in a couple of days. You'll have everything you need."

"Why Neapolis?" Lucius asks as our parents' three carriages arrive.

"Because it's safe," I reply. I tell him goodbye and close the door. Behind me, the servants carry out the last of my belongings.

Fiona and I walk over to the carriage holding my mother and father. Mother leans out the window as I approach. "Marcus!"

"Good morning, Mother," I say, stepping closer. "Good morning, Father."

"We will see you in a day or two?" he asks.

"Yes," I say. "Find a home, and we'll meet you there."

Fiona steps up beside me. "Safe travels."

My mother's expression softens. "And the two of you be careful as well." She reaches through the window and squeezes my hand.

"I will," I say, squeezing back before letting go.

I step away with Fiona and signal the drivers. The carriages begin to roll forward together into the first light of the sunrise.

We head back into the house to get Felix. I step into the hallway, bend down, and scratch behind his ears. "Come on, Felix. It's time to go," I say, and he follows eagerly.

When I return to the doorway, Fiona is waiting. "We should grab something to eat at the forum while we decide the best way to get the message out."

She nods. "That's a great idea."

As we begin our walk, I turn to Fiona. "I've been wondering, why do you still speak Oscan in your time? They still use our language thousands of years in the future?"

She laughs. "No, actually. I learned it because I was studying your city. I usually speak a language called English."

"English?" I repeat, intrigued. "Will you speak some for me? Please?"

She grins. "All right... *That dog of yours is very clever.*"

I frown, trying to catch the meaning. The words are very strange. I ask her what she said, and when she translates, I'm surprised.

"That's humorous," I say with a wink. "How do you say... 'I love Marcus'?"

Fiona giggles and says the phrase in English.

"I made you say it," I admit, still beaming.

"You didn't make me," she replies, smiling. "I would've said it anyway."

Her words make me smile so much that my face begins to hurt. I pull her close and kiss her soundly.

We continue walking until we reach a bakery.

"I'll get us something to eat," I say, stepping inside. I order bread and cheese, and some dried meat for Felix. While I'm there, I ask the baker if he's planning on moving to the new location, and he confirms that he is. Another family will be saved.

I hand Fiona her breakfast, and she takes it with a grateful smile. I toss a bite to Felix, who catches it in his mouth and wags his tail.

We find a shade tree, ready to start planning while we eat. Once we have something solid in mind, we head to the stables.

When Felix, Fiona, and I arrive, a few riders are already saddling their horses for the day's errands. I call out, "Would anyone like to make some coin? If you do, please come over here!"

Within minutes, half a dozen teenage boys stand before us, eyes filled with curiosity.

"This is urgent," I tell them. "I need riders to take messages to Herculaneum, Stabiae, Oplontis, Boscoreale, and Nuceria. Tell everyone in each town that the festival tonight in the northwestern meadow near the vineyards is in their honor. Tell them that we are honoring their cities with ours and with exciting performances. We would love for their performers and sellers to join us there. There's plenty of room. Everyone in each town must know. You can't let a single person miss out. Do you understand?"

"I understand," says a wiry boy. "I'll take Herculaneum."

"I'll go to Stabiae," another says.

"I'll go to Oplontis," adds a third.

By the time I reach into my pouch and start handing out coins, I have volunteers for every small village in the countryside.

"Now, ride quickly, and make sure they all hear. Don't leave anyone out. This is very important. Then you need to get yourselves to the festival as well."

The boys nod, scatter to prepare their horses, and ride off in different directions.

As the boys disappear into the streets, I turn to Fiona. "Which of the cities do you think will be hit the worst when Vesuvius erupts?"

"Herculaneum," she says. "It's closer. It will be the first to be destroyed."

I nod. "Follow me," I say.

We approach the stable manager. "I need a carriage and horses," I say, reaching into my pouch. "I'll pay well for their use, just for today."

He studies me, looks at the amount of coin I'm offering, and then nods. "It will be ready at once, Dominus."

Within the hour, a carriage hitched to two strong horses pulls up. I help Fiona inside, Felix climbs in next to her, and I close the door.

After climbing into the driver's seat, I take the reins. "Hold tight," I call to Fiona.

The road to Herculaneum winds down the slopes. I keep my eyes on the path. Having dealt with the magistrate before, I remember where he lives and drive straight to his house. Even though I already sent a rider here, I want to extend the invitation myself just in case. It takes almost three hours to get there, but it's worth it.

I leap down first, help Fiona out, and tell Felix to stay, closing the carriage door behind us.

We approach the front door, and I raise my hand and knock. The door opens, and a servant stands before us. "Good day," he says.

"Good day. I am Marcus Valerius, aedile of Pompeii, responsible for organizing the festival for Jupiter and Venus," I say. "This is my companion, Fiona. I have come to speak with the magistrate about an honor for your town."

The servant steps back, inclining his head. "Please, come inside." Fiona and I follow the servant into the magistrate's atrium. Sunlight pours down through the open roof above the impluvium. "I will fetch the magistrate," he says, bowing before hurrying away.

A few moments pass before the magistrate enters. He's a tall man, wearing fresh robes, and his expression is curious but polite. "Valerius, " he says. "Wonderful to see you again."

"It's good to see you as well, Magistrate. This is my companion, Fiona," I reply.

"Fiona, it's a pleasure to meet you," he says. "Now, to what do I owe the honor of your visit?"

"I have come to speak with you about tonight's festival. It will be held in the meadow near the vineyards, and tonight is in honor of *your* people. Your village will be honored with special performances celebrating Herculaneum. It is an event that should not be missed."

The magistrate studies me for a moment, and then a smile spreads across his face. "In our honor?"

"Yes," I say. "Jupiter and Venus have seen fit to honor you in this festival, and your presence is requested. The performances, the celebrations—it is all for your people."

He nods, clearly pleased. "I will see that everyone knows. This is… most generous of Pompeii, Valerius."

"I am glad you accept our invitation," I reply. "Every citizen should know—no one should miss it."

The magistrate nods. "It will be done. You have my word."

Fiona and I rise to leave, and a wave of pride crashes over me. Perhaps we can save everyone who might have fallen victim to Vesuvius's wrath.

As we walk back to the carriage, I look at Fiona. "Now what?" I ask.

She smiles as I help her inside. "Now we take the stage and make an announcement."

Driving away from Herculaneum, I consider my words, turning them over carefully in my mind. How am I going to tell thousands of people that Vesuvius will soon rain ash down on them, that they must flee their homes and leave everything behind?

21

WARNING!

FIONA

Back at the festival, Marcus and I watch the last performances of the night take the stage. Felix sits between us, resting his head in my lap. People from the neighboring villages have arrived, and most of those who live in Pompeii are here, too. There are thousands in the audience, which means the first part of our plan worked. We got nearly everyone to come to the celebration where Marcus will soon make his announcement.

"Do you know what you're going to say when you get up there?" I ask. "Have you thought about how they might react?"

"I've thought about it quite a bit," he says. "And yet, I still don't have any idea of how this will go. I'm… nervous."

"Don't be nervous," I say. "You're going to save many lives, and whatever happens, you're not alone."

He smiles at me, and I squeeze his arm. The music winds to its final note, and applause rolls through the meadow. Marcus crouches beside Felix and ruffles his ears. "Stay with Fiona," he says quietly. The dog obeys, nuzzling my hand, his tail thumping the ground.

Then Marcus straightens, takes a deep breath, and steps toward the stage. I watch him go, a knot of anxiety and awe twisting in my chest. He's so incredibly brave; I don't know that I could do what he's about to do.

Marcus steps onto the stage and raises his voice. "I need to make an announcement, and I need everyone to hear me. If you can hear me—pass this message backward to those who can't hear my voice."

A ripple of attention moves through the crowd. People get quiet, lean forward, and rise to see and hear him clearly.

He swallows, glances over the thousands of faces before him, then continues. "At midday tomorrow, something terrible will happen. As I share this miserable fate, I need you all to remain calm."

The murmurs start low at first, questions floating up from the crowd. Heads turn, people exchange anxious glances, and some call out, asking for clarity.

Marcus holds up a hand to quiet them. "Listen carefully. Do *not* go home tonight! Stay here, or make your way to Neapolis. Your cities will not survive until tomorrow night."

The questions grow louder, and more urgent. People are pointing, calling to friends and family, trying to figure out what Marcus means. He raises his voice again. "Vesuvius is going to erupt! The mountain will turn to fire and ash, which will rain down over our villages! All of your cities will be destroyed, and everyone in them will die! Do not go back! Remain here or go to Neapolis."

Panic licks through the crowd like the wave of ash that will descend in a few days. Shouts and cries break out across the meadow. Some push through the crowd, some freeze in shock, and others clutch their children. A few scream that he is a liar, that he should be punished for frightening them.

I watch Marcus face the shouting, the accusations, and the fear spilling out in every direction. The crowd is anxious, angry, and desperate. I feel all of their emotions at once, and it's overwhelming. Yet, I can't just sit here while people risk going home.

Marcus continues to plead with the crowd as I stand, taking a shaky step forward, then another, climbing onto the stage beside him. My voice trembles at first. "Listen to me! He's not lying! What he's saying is true! I know this is hard to believe, but if you go home tonight, you won't make it to tomorrow. Stay here, or make your way to Neapolis. Please, do not go back into your cities! Some of you have already felt the ground trembling these past few days. You know that is a sign from the gods."

A few people call out, demanding proof, asking why they should trust me.

"We sent word to all of your villages today inviting you here so that we could save you! We wouldn't do that if it wasn't an emergency! I can only tell you what I know. Vesuvius will erupt, and your cities will be covered in flames and ash. Everyone in them will die! You must *not* go home tonight. If you believe me, what have you got to lose? One night in a beautiful meadow? Why not believe me?"

Slowly, more people begin to listen. They stop shouting and look between Marcus and me, trying to understand. I realize the reason they're listening to me must be my appearance. The fact that I'm different from them is causing them to be curious enough to hear me out.

A voice cuts through the chaos. "What about our animals? We can't just leave them!"

"If you must return for your animals, do it now!" he shouts. "Then come back here to the meadow. Bring all of your animals, your elderly, your servants, and return here immediately. At midday tomorrow, your homes will be gone. Everyone in them will die!"

Tension crashes over the crowd. People shout to one another, debating whether to risk returning to their homes. Some push forward, trying to make the dangerous trip to gather family members and animals they left behind, before it's too late.

When we step down from the stage, my body begins vibrating from the adrenaline. Felix waits for us at the edge of the stage, and I kneel to pet him, unsure whether I'm reassuring him or myself.

"Do you think most of them listened to our warning?" I ask Marcus.

"It's difficult to tell. All we could do was give them the choice," he replies.

"We did the best we could," I agree as he leads Felix and me to the treeline.

The crowd thins as people rush back toward the cities, leaving gaps that make the meadow feel larger and emptier. Families who remain find places to rest, spreading blankets and huddling together. I watch them, silently praying that those who left did so to either head for Neapolis or to gather loved ones and return here to safety. I pray that they didn't return home because they didn't believe Marcus and me. Every figure disappearing into the dark makes my stomach churn with worry, and I can only hope everyone survives.

Once we are in the trees, away from the disarray of the meadow, we find a patch of smooth ground where we can lie down. Felix curls up at our feet, and I stretch out next to Marcus.

My eyelids are heavy, and I know that even with all that's going on around us, I'll be asleep within minutes. Just as I begin to fall asleep, I hear a child's voice. "Dominus…"

We sit up instantly. Marcus speaks into the shadows. "Who is there?"

"Dominus, it is I, Decimus." The boy steps closer, hesitating.

Marcus stands. "What is it? Are you hurt?"

Decimus swallows hard and glances down at the ground. "I'm not hurt. It's my grandmother… she's at home in the city, and I don't know what to do."

Marcus asks. "Do you have any way of getting her to safety?"

"No, Dominus. She's very old and frail." The boy begins to cry.

Marcus stands and puts his arms around Decimus. "Don't worry," he says in a gentle voice. "We'll figure it out. Let's go find someone with a carriage."

I rise and follow Marcus and Decimus, Felix walking next to me. We move through the meadow, looking for anyone with a wagon or carriage. Marcus calls out to a man tending a wagon, "Excuse me, could I rent your wagon and team for a short trip? I'll pay handsomely."

The man shrugs. "I'll lend it to you for free—if you bring it back before dawn."

Marcus nods. "We'll most definitely return it before dawn." He reaches into his pouch anyway and drops a few coins into the man's hand. "For your trouble."

The man tucks the coins away, nods again, and steps aside. "Very well. Be quick."

Marcus holds out his hand, and I climb into the driver's seat, sliding over. Once I'm safely up, he swings himself onto the bench beside me. Decimus jumps into the bed of the wagon, and Felix following him. Marcus takes the reins, nudges the horses forward, and we start moving toward Pompeii. I lean back, fighting exhaustion and trying to stay awake as he drives.

Once we enter the streets of Pompeii, Marcus glances back at the boy. "Decimus, can you give me directions to your house?"

He nods, pointing down a nearby street. "First left here, then straight past the fountain. My house is the second one on the right, the one with the stone fence. Grandma will be inside."

Marcus guides the wagon carefully, weaving between people rushing through the streets, carrying bundles, guiding animals, and calling out to one another. The noise of shouting, clattering carts, and footsteps fills the air. We push forward, following Decimus's directions, until we reach the house with the stone fence just as he described. Marcus brings the horses to a stop.

Leaning over the side of the wagon, Marcus says, "Decimus, go inside and bring out as many blankets and pillows as you can find. Put them in the empty space in the bed of the wagon." The man we borrowed the wagon from has entrusted us with many of his belongings, it seems. He must be one of the shop owners who brought his wares to sell.

Decimus nods and hurries toward the house.

Marcus slides down from the wagon. "Felix, stay," he says, and the dog sits obediently by the wagon.

Marcus helps me down, and together, we follow Decimus into the house. He leads us to his grandmother's bed. Marcus crouches beside her. "We need to get you out of the city," he says. "There will be danger tomorrow. Decimus and I are here to take you somewhere safe."

She looks at us, weak and confused. "Danger…?" she whispers.

"Yes," I say gently, stepping closer. "We need to take you some-where safe. You don't have to walk. We'll help you."

She murmurs something I don't quite catch and then lets out a shaky sigh.

"Can I help you up?" Marcus asks.

She nods weakly, and Marcus lifts her easily into his arms as Decimus and I gather pillows and blankets. We hurry out ahead of Marcus, tossing them into the bed of the wagon, creating a soft place for Marcus to lay the elderly woman. He lowers her gently onto the pile.

"Decimus, where is the rest of your family?" Marcus asks.

"It's just grandmother and me," he replies, his voice weak.

My heart aches for the child, and I can see in Marcus's face that he, too, is touched by the fact that Decimus is not only raising himself but taking care of his grandmother alone.

We load up, and Marcus drives the wagon back to the meadow. Once we reach the treeline, we move to the spot where we had planned to sleep and arrange the blankets and pillows on the ground. Marcus lifts the woman carefully and lays her onto the pile. Then Decimus lies down beside her, and Felix curls up on his other side.

"I'll return the wagon," Marcus says. "I'll be right back."

I nod. "Be careful," I tell him.

I lie down next to Felix and wait for Marcus to return. Decimus whispers, "Thank you for your help," as he drifts off to sleep, and I reach over to brush his hair from his face. He deserves our help. His grandmother deserves our help. Everyone in the shadow of Vesuvius deserves to live. I just hope they listened, that they believe, and that tomorrow, they all make the right choice and flee before it's too late.

Marcus returns quietly, lying down on the blankets beside me. He leans over and kisses my forehead. "Good night," he murmurs.

"Good night," I whisper back.

I feel him getting comfortable next to me, the protection of his presence calming, and before I even realize it, sleep takes me.

22

LIFE AND DEATH

MARCUS

I wake at dawn to the sounds of movement in the meadow—footsteps, arguments, children crying, and dogs barking. People are waking, packing, arguing over where they should go, and trying to figure out how to escape the mountain before it blows.

I shake Fiona gently. "Wake up. We have to move."

She opens her eyes. "Is it already morning?"

"Yes, and I think the first thing we should do is find Decimus and his grandmother a way to Neapolis."

The boy stirs, groggy, and rubs his eyes. "Neapolis?"

"Yes, Decimus. It's the safest place for you right now. You stay here with your grandmother," I say firmly. "Fiona and I will see what we can find."

The little boy nods and stays put, his grandmother still asleep next to him. Fiona and Felix follow me as I push through the restless crowd, looking for the man with the wagon we borrowed last night.

When I find him, he's finishing tending his team of horses. His wife and three children sit in the wagon, ready to leave, and I give them a friendly wave.

"Do you remember me? From last night?" I ask.

"Of course I do," he says, eyes twinkling. "You told everyone the world was about to be on fire… and then borrowed my wagon."

I bite back a laugh at his blunt way with words. "Yes, that was me," I say. "We were wondering if you're heading to Neapolis?"

"We are," he says, nodding. "If what you say is true, we'll be safe there. And if you're lying, we can always return once we know it's safe."

"You're a sensible man," I reply. "I assumed as much last night, and now I see it's true. I have another favor to ask."

He raises an eyebrow, curiosity sparking in his gaze. "Go on."

"There's a young boy whose only family is his grandmother. She can't walk, but he cares for her. They need a ride to Neapolis. I borrowed your wagon to go back for her last night. I'll pay whatever you ask if you'll take them there for me."

He glances at his wife and then back at me. "I'm going to Neapolis anyway. You don't have to pay me. Bring me the boy and the woman," he says, his sensible bluntness shining through again.

"Thank you. That's very kind of you," I reply. "I'll return shortly."

Fiona, Felix, and I make our way back to the treeline where we left Decimus and his grandmother. I crouch beside him. "There are kind people who've offered to give you a ride. And when I get to the city, I'll find you, Decimus. Don't worry—you'll be safe."

"Thank you, Dominus," Decimus says softly. "You've been so kind to me."

"Decimus, you helped save my brother. I'll always take care of you," I say.

He nods, brushing a tear from his cheek.

His grandmother stirs, looks at us, and says, "You are a good man, Dominus. The gods will bless you."

"I'm glad I am able to help you," I assure her. I lift her from the blankets. She holds onto my shoulder. "I've got you. You're all right," I murmur. The woman wraps her arms around my neck, letting me carry her more easily.

When we get back to the family with the wagon, I wait for Decimus to place some blankets down and then gently place the old woman in the wagon bed. The boy hops in beside her and introduces himself to the family. They all seem to take to him immediately, and I feel he's in good hands.

Before leaving, I say, "I'm Marcus Valerius. When I arrive in Neapolis, I will find you and retrieve the boy and his grandmother. May I have your name?"

The man smiles, nodding once. "I'm Caius Septimius. Don't worry, Valerius. They'll be safe with us."

I nod as the man climbs into the driver's seat and pulls the wagon forward just as the sun rises fully.

"Goodbye, Decimus! We'll see you soon!" Fiona calls, and we both wave to the boy who frantically waves back.

I turn to Fiona. "Can you believe we only have a few hours left?"

She shakes her head, looking up at the mountain. "Mere hours."

"I think we should go back into the city one last time," I say. "Urge anyone still there to leave."

She takes my hand. "Agreed."

We leave the meadow behind and follow the path toward the city, catching a ride with a man who is on his way to look for his brother. Smoke puffs from the slopes of Vesuvius, gray and heavy in the morning sky, and a tremor shudders through the ground beneath our feet. Ash drifts down in light, powdery flakes.

The closer we get to the city, the more people we see already moving out—families in wagons piled with belongings.

"At least some of them are leaving," Fiona says.

"That's a good start." I nod, feeling the air thicken with heat and a sulfur tang that makes our noses wrinkle.

From the forested hills above the city, a herd of deer bursts into motion, pounding down the slopes, eyes wide with terror. Felix growls softly and moves closer to me, tail stiff, ears forward. Normally, he would chase after them, barking and yipping with excitement. The fact that he isn't tells me everything I need to know —something is *very* wrong.

"See that?" I say. "Even the animals know it isn't safe."

Fiona nods. "We need to hurry."

The man driving the carriage spurs the horses on faster.

When we reach the city, the streets are a blur of motion. People are moving quickly toward the gates, helping children and the elderly, holding what they can carry. Others carry on as if it's any other morning, sweeping doorways, carrying baskets, opening shops—ignoring the ash in the air and the tremors underfoot. They aren't alarmed. They seem to be refusing to acknowledge the danger.

"We need to reach those who won't leave," I say. "They don't understand yet."

We hop off the carriage and weave through the crowd until we reach a woman with a baby on her hip as she stoops to fill a clay jar at the fountain. Her other child tugs at her skirts, just as a tremor shakes the stone streets.

"Domina," I say gently, "you need to leave. Now."

She glances up at us, frowning. "Leave? I can't just abandon my home. The children—"

Fiona steps closer. "We've seen the ash drifting down from the mountain. We've seen the deer fleeing the slopes. Vesuvius is going to erupt, and it will kill everyone in the city."

At that moment, a flock of birds bursts from the trees near the mountain, screeching as they wheel into the sky, fleeing as if they can sense the danger. The woman's eyes widen with fear, following the birds, the color draining from her face. Her baby fusses on her hip.

"Oh... oh no," she whispers.

"Yes," Fiona says firmly. "You need to get your family and go. Take what you can carry. Head to Neapolis as fast as you can."

She nods. "All right... all right. Thank you."

"Move quickly. Every second matters," I add.

We keep moving down the street, and the ash drifting thicker makes my eyes water. Felix stays close, low to the ground, sniffing, his back rigid.

Near the next fountain, we see a man sitting on the edge, looking hopeless, tears streaking his face.

Fiona jogs over. "Dominus! What's wrong? Why are you crying?"

He shakes his head, trepidation clear. "I… I can't leave. No one will help me."

I walk over and crouch, glancing at his legs. "Can you walk?"

He shakes his head, voice trembling. "I'm paralyzed. I can't leave by myself. Everyone else is going, and I'm stuck here."

Fiona kneels beside him. "You'll be all right. We'll figure this out. We'll find you a ride out of the city. Felix will stay right here and watch over you."

I tell my dog to stay, and he obediently sits at the man's feet, as if he understands that this is life or death.

Fiona and I step out into the street, searching for anyone heading to Neapolis. The first carriage we spot looks like it belongs to a wealthy household. I raise my hand and signal the driver to stop. "Excuse me," I call, stepping forward, "are you traveling to Neapolis?"

The man pops his head out of the carriage window, and I move closer to speak with him. "Yes, we are," he says. "After the mountain started rumbling and the animals went wild, we decided you were right—we should get out of here."

"I need a favor," I say, leaning closer. "There's a man—he can't walk on his own. He needs a ride out of the city. Can you take him with you?"

The man frowns and shakes his head. "No. We're already crowded enough, and that's asking too much. We can't—"

"Are you serious?" I snap, exasperated.

Fiona steps forward, her eyes blazing. "Did you not hear the call at the festival? Do you not feel the eyes of the gods and goddesses on us now? Every priest, priestess, and every deity we honor—they demand we help those who can't help themselves. This isn't about fear or convenience. It's about living or dying. You turn your back on him, and you turn your back on what we all swore to uphold."

The woman leans out of the carriage window, startled, her frown softening. "We'll help the man. Where is he?"

"There," I say, pointing down the street. "We can lead you to him."

Her husband nods reluctantly. "All right. We'll help him. Let's go."

We lead the carriage back to the fountain. The man is sitting where we left him, his face lighting up the moment he sees us. "You came back," he chokes out, his voice thick with emotion.

"Of course," I say, kneeling to lift him off the ground as Fiona helps him from the other side. "We found someone who can take you to safety."

We carry him to the wealthy man's carriage and help him inside.

Once he's settled, the lame man smiles at us. "Thank you. Truly."

"Be safe," Fiona says, placing her hand on his shoulder. "Go quickly."

The carriage pulls away, and I glance around. "Wait..." My stomach drops. "Where's Felix?"

"Felix?" Fiona yells, scanning the street. "He was right here a moment ago..."

Panic burns through me. "We can't leave him behind!"

"Of course we can't leave him behind," Fiona says, her voice frantic with worry.

I spin, running down the street, stopping to look in every alley that he could be hiding in. "Felix!" I roar, my voice cracking with desperation. "Come! Now!"

Fiona runs down the opposite side of the street, shouting, "Felix! Where are you?!"

I stop, whip around, and my eyes dart across the street. My heart aches. "Felix!" I whistle for him. "Felix!" I whistle again, louder this time.

Every moment that passes, the city becomes more dangerous. It also feels impossibly large, every sound swallowed by the low rumble of the mountain, ash drifting over rooftops, coating everything in gray. My stomach turns over as I keep running between carts and barrels, scanning every corner. "Felix!"

Fiona runs over to me. "Has he ever done this before?" she asks.

I shake my head, frustration and fear twisting together. "No—he's never run away. He's been with me since he was a puppy! He's my best friend, Fiona... I can't—"

A whimper and a short bark hit my ear from down the street. "Felix?" I call.

Another bark, closer this time, louder and more urgent. I grab Fiona's arm. "That must be him!"

We follow the sound, weaving between people and abandoned goods. He comes into view, crouched protectively next to a little girl, who can't be more than five.

"Felix!" I shout, rushing forward. The dog's tail wags furiously as he looks up at me. Relief floods my chest. "Good boy! Who did you find?"

The little girl peers up at me, shaking and scared. "I got all turned around," she says, her voice small and scared.

Fiona kneels, smiling at her. "Do you know where you live?"

"No," the child whispers, looking down at her feet. "I can't find my mama."

From somewhere behind us, a frightened voice yells. "Octavia! Where are you?!"

The girl's eyes light up. "Mama!" she cries, running toward the woman as she barrels through the street.

When she reaches her child, the woman scoops her up, hugging her tightly. "Oh, thank the gods, I found you!"

I look down at Felix. "You found Octavia, didn't you?" I say, scratching him behind his ears. Felix yips, nudging me with his nose.

Fiona pets him, too. "Good dog, Felix. You're always looking out for others."

I squeeze Felix tight, my heart still pounding. "I thought I'd lost you for a second."

"Thank you for finding her," the woman says as she runs back out into the street with her little girl in her arms.

"Stay safe! Leave the city!" I yell after them.

I look up at Vesuvius as it rumbles again, and then turn to Fiona. "Let's get out of here."

23

THE WOMAN WHO SAVED POMPEII

FIONA

Marcus and I have been running from Vesuvius for what feels like days now, but I am sure it's only been a couple of hours. Felix never leaves Marcus's side as we alternate between jogging and walking, knowing we are running out of time before Vesuvius erupts. We are desperate to put as much distance between ourselves and the mountain as possible.

As we head down the road toward Neapolis, which is present-day Naples, I see families moving in every direction: riding in wagons, on horses, and many people are on foot like us. I feel a surge of pride at how many lives Marcus and I were able to save. Still, thinking of those who refused to leave, I know there will be victims we couldn't convince in time.

We slow our pace when we're about halfway to Naples, which should take us between four and six hours, depending upon how clogged the road is with other people fleeing, and Marcus hands me his canteen. I take a drink and then hand it back.

"It might be difficult to find your people when we get into the city," I say. "Neapolis is going to be overflowing."

"People will work together to locate their loved ones," he says, his voice calm. "It will be all right."

The ground shudders violently. Felix scrambles and topples over, and I stumble into Marcus, who catches me and helps me find my footing so I don't fall.

Another shake has us stumbling, and it's harder this time. Felix growls, his fur bristling, and lies down flat. Dust kicks up around our feet as the roar of the mountain bursts into the sky.

People ahead are screaming now. Carts tip, spilling bundles and children, parents scooping them up, dragging them to their feet. "Move faster! Keep moving!" someone shouts.

From the treeline, a small herd of wild boars bursts into a nearby clearing. They dart away from the forest, moving fast, and for a moment, the people running past catch sight of them and shriek in surprise. Felix dashes toward the edge of the path, barking, then spins back to us, eyes wild.

A tremor knocks me sideways. I stumble into Marcus again. Ahead, a woman trips over a fallen bundle, screaming that she's hurt her leg, and a man bends to help her up.

The sky behind us, near the mountain, glows orange and red. Ash drifts down like snow, coating faces, hair, and the fields on either side of the road. Birds erupt from the trees in shrill clouds, wings beating frantically. Small animals burst from the forest, scattering in all directions.

I clutch Marcus's arm. "It's happening!"

"We better keep moving," he says, taking my hand and pulling me along.

The mountain screams behind us, and still the road stretches ahead, filled with desperate, frightened people. Every step is a fight, every second is sheer chaos. I drop Marcus's hand to run faster and force my legs to carry me, knowing we can't stop now.

We run another two or three miles before finally slowing to catch our breath. The further we run, the weaker the tremors feel, the ground only occasionally shuddering beneath our feet. The screams ahead are replaced by the chatter of hurried conversation—still tense, but no longer raw panic.

"I... I think the crowd is growing more calm." I gasp as we slow to a brisk walk.

He nods. "We're getting farther away, and they know they're fleeing to safety."

Dust and ash swirl around us. People are still moving, but the stampede has calmed. I glance back. The smoke and fire-red glow from Vesuvius still hang over the horizon, but the roar is distant now.

Finally, after moving for about five hours, judging from the location of the sun in the southwestern horizon, Marcus and I approach the outskirts of Neapolis.

The road narrows as more people converge here—those fleeing Pompeii and nearby villages, mixing with the locals who are most likely utterly confused. The noise is still loud but less frenzied than it was closer to Vesuvius. Voices shout to one another, and wagons jostle as families make their way into the city to begin their new lives.

"This place is just as packed as I'd imagined it would be," I say, wiping sweat from my brow. "How do we even move through? Let alone find your family?"

Marcus scans the throngs of people. "Yes, this is quite intense. I say we find a place to stay for tonight and figure the rest out tomorrow."

"Marcus, I don't think there's any room at the inn." I know he won't understand my Christian reference, but that's okay. I am serious, after all. I giggle under my breath. Despite everything, I can't help it.

He looks around. "You're right about that." After a beat, he says, "Wait... how is that funny?"

I laugh and shake my head as we continue down the street, trying to find a place to rest. "I'll explain some other time."

"I'm starving," Marcus says. "Let's at least find some food."

"I'm hungry, too. I just realized we haven't even eaten yet today," I reply.

Marcus and I walk until we spot a tavern tucked between two

larger buildings. When the door swings open, we immediately smell the warm bread and roasted meat.

"Thank the gods," Marcus mutters. He orders bread, meat, and wine. As the owner heads back to fetch our food, Marcus steps outside to fill our canteen at the fountain. He returns just as the man brings our lunch, and we find a table and dig in, sharing hunks of meat and sips of water with Felix. I gulp down the water and wine, eating more than I have in days.

"I feel so much better," I say when I've finished.

"I'm glad you feel better." He wipes his mouth on a napkin and takes a deep breath. "I'm so happy I met you, Fiona. You saved thousands of people. How can I be so fortunate to love the woman who saved Pompeii?"

I blush at the idea of someone thinking of me as someone who saved an entire city. "I'm just me—Fiona Lockwood."

"Fiona Lockwood?" he says, almost like it's a question.

"Yes, that's my last name," I reply.

"I like it," he says, smiling.

"Thank you." I chuckle. Have I never told him my last name?

"Well, Fiona Lockwood, what would you like to do first—look for my family or find a place to sleep tonight?"

"Well," I say, smiling at him, "maybe if we find one, we'll find the other."

Marcus laughs. "Let's start here. I'll ask the restaurant owner."

Marcus and I approach the counter, and the man who prepared our food looks up. "Do you know of a family by the name of Valerius? They just moved to town."

"No, Dominus," he replies. "I'm sorry, but it seems like a great many people have just recently moved to town."

"Thank you anyway," Marcus says, handing him some coins.

He nods. "I hope you find them."

"Thank you," I say as we step out through the tavern doors.

Once we're back out on the street, Marcus leans toward me. "We'll check the places they might have already shopped. The bakery, butcher, fruit stalls—and then we'll move toward the market."

At the bakery, Marcus asks the baker, "Have you met the Valerius family? They just moved here."

The baker shakes his head. "There's an older couple named Valerius, but they've lived here all their lives."

Marcus frowns. "They must be distant relatives. Thank you," he says politely as we step out of the shop. I wonder why he doesn't ask where they live. Maybe that's the family his mother mentioned.

We move to the fruit stalls. "Excuse me," I call to a vendor. "Have you met Dominus Valerius? Lucius Valerius?"

Everyone shrugs or shakes their head.

I glance at Marcus as we move down the street. "Maybe we should try whoever keeps track of property," I suggest. "Someone there might know if your family has bought a house recently."

"Why didn't I think of that myself?" he asks, shaking his head. "Of course. Let's go to the local magistrate."

Felix stays close to Marcus as he leads us through the streets.

"Do you really think he will know anything?" I ask.

"He should," Marcus says. "Even just a note, a scribal record, or a mention by a negotiator. If anyone knows where my parents and Lucius live, it will be someone in this office."

We turn a corner and spot a modest office, its steps crowded with people coming and going.

"This is the place," Marcus says, stopping in front of the building. "Property transactions are recorded here—sales, purchases, and leases."

Marcus turns to Felix. "Wait here, Felix. Stay."

Felix lies down, and Marcus and I walk up the steps and inside the office. In the main room, people are working at desks, filling out forms, talking quietly, and exchanging papers.

We make our way toward the receptionist area, and that's when I spot him and can't hold back. "Look, Marcus, it's Quintus!"

I see Cornelia is sitting beside him, the children playing at their feet.

Marcus pushes through the crowd. "Quintus!" he calls.

"Marcus! Fiona!" Quintus says. "I'm so glad you made it. We were so worried. We thought you'd stay too long trying to save more people."

"We made it out alive. It's so good to see you! I'm so glad you're all safe," Marcus says.

Cornelia wipes her eyes, laughing softly. "We weren't sure you had escaped. Seeing you here…" She shakes her head. "It's a miracle."

Once the initial surprise subsides, Marcus asks. "What are you all doing here?"

Quintus smiles. "We're buying a house," he says proudly. "We're just starting the process, and we're about to go to our new home."

"Congratulations!" I say.

Marcus grins. "Yes, congratulations indeed."

"Thank you," Quintus says. "If it wasn't for you, we'd still be in Pompeii right now…" He trails off, and for a moment, we all fall silent, thinking of what might have happened if they hadn't left.

"Everyone we love is safe now," Cornelia says, lifting little Julia into her arms and tousling Gaius's curls.

"Yes, and that's what's most important now," I say, smiling at her. "Would the two of you happen to know where Marcus's family settled down? Do you know if they were able to purchase a home here yet?"

Quintus smiles. "Actually, we do. We went to look at a house for sale we were considering, but they bought it first."

"What's the address?" Marcus asks excitedly.

"Solarius Street," Quintus says. "Two-story house, pale yellow façade, and a large wooden door. Just past the fountain."

"It's very large and lovely," Cornelia adds. "The gardens are gorgeous, filled with blooms."

"Thank you," Marcus says. "And where is your new house?"

"We're on Livia Street, not far from the market. A red-brick house with green shutters. Please, come and visit us soon."

"We'll visit very soon," Marcus says. "But now, Fiona and I need to see if we can find my family."

Quintus nods. "Of course. Be careful."

I step forward. "Goodbye," I say, giving Cornelia a quick hug.

"Goodbye, Julia. Goodbye, Gaius," Marcus adds. "See you soon."

We turn and move through the room toward the door. Back outside, the sun begins to set over Neapolis as we make our way to Solarius Street, hand in hand, Felix sticking close. We're no longer in a hurry and no longer fleeing terror or disaster.

I look over at Marcus and realize that even if we couldn't save everyone in Pompeii, even if I *can't* make it back to my own time, what truly matters is that he and I found each other and that we made it out alive. We did the best we could to save as many people as possible, and at the end of the longest day of my life, that's all I can ask for.

2 4

BY THE GODS

MARCUS

A month has passed since we arrived in Neapolis. The city is over-flowing with people who fled Pompeii and the surrounding villages after the mountain erupted.

The home I grew up in is rubble. The house I lived in with my dog and my servants is dust. So many people didn't make it out of the city... and yet, my family is safe. My servants are safe. Most of the people I know made it out alive because they trusted me, and I only knew what to do because I trusted Fiona. I can't stop thinking about how close we all came to death and how much depended on the giant leaps of faith and acts of courage.

I found my family and Quintus on the very first day we arrived. My mother and father love Fiona. They know she saved their lives—and their sons' lives—but that's not why they love her. Fiona is lovable because she is kind, selfless, strong, and giving. Even my brother Lucius has asked me what I did to deserve her. Honestly, I don't know. All I can do is be grateful for her and for the way she puts up with me.

During our first week in the city, we tracked down Decimus and his grandmother. Fiona insists that we raise the boy and care for his

173

grandmother so he can have a proper childhood. Every day, she amazes me.

I've started working as an archivist, organizing records and cataloging the city's documents. It's not too exciting, but it keeps me occupied and focused. And through it all, Fiona has been by my side. I can't imagine doing any of this without her. Every morning, I look over at her and realize how much she means to me.

Fiona and I picked a house large enough for Decimus, his grandmother, whose name is Junia, and anyone else Fiona chooses to help. It's a two-story building with sturdy stone walls and a red-tiled roof. The front door opens into a bright main room with high ceilings, and the windows let in plenty of sunlight. Upstairs, there are several rooms—enough for guests, family, and anyone who needs shelter. It feels solid, safe, and big enough to grow into, just like the life we're building here. There's even a large garden out back with enough space for flowers, herbs, and vegetables.

After all Fiona and I have been through, and after all the ways she's shown me her softness and her strength, today, I'm finally going to marry the woman I love.

"Marcus, are you ready?" Quintus's voice cuts in, pulling me back from my thoughts.

I look at him. "Yes. I'm ready, Quintus."

He grins. "Good. Let's not keep them waiting."

Quintus and I step into the flower garden, where bright blooms fill every bed. Guests are already seated. My parents are in the front row, and Lucius sits beside them. Cornelia holds Julia, Gaius squirming at her feet, and Quintus takes his seat with his family. Decimus is here, watching over Felix toward the back of the garden, and I stand at the front with the priest, waiting for Fiona. She explained to me how weddings are held in her time, and we've done what we can to make it similar to what she's always dreamed about, even if it's a bit different than what I'm used to.

The small ensemble strikes up a soft tune with a slow tempo, and I look at the door Fiona will come through. My pulse races as it opens, and there she stands.

Fiona is stunning in her light pink tunic, her yellow flammeum brushing her shoulders. As she gets closer, and I look into her beautiful sky-blue eyes, I feel as though everything I've ever wanted or needed in the world is falling into place.

FIONA

As I walk through the garden toward Marcus, I can't believe how far we've come—how far I've come. I traveled back two thousand years for this man. I stood by his side through the world's worst natural disaster, and in just a few more steps, I'll stand before our friends and family and pledge my life to him.

When I reach the front, I stand next to Marcus, and he takes my hand. As the last few notes of the song fade out, Marcus looks at me with love in his eyes, and I melt.

The priest lifts his voice. "Marcus, do you accept Fiona to be your wife, to share your life and honor the gods?"

"I do," Marcus replies. His hand tightens around mine.

"And you, Fiona, do you accept Marcus to be your husband, to share his life and honor the gods?"

"I do," I answer.

The priest lifts our joined hands. "By the gods, you are now husband and wife."

Our guests clap, and Marcus looks at me, giving me the most handsome smile I've ever seen. I still can't believe I'm his wife. Our lives together shouldn't even be possible, yet here we are on our wedding day.

We hold the reception in the garden under a large tent. Our guests enjoy our best wine, and a wonderful spread of Italian food fills the tables. Everyone dances— even little Julia and Gaius.

As we sit at the head table, plates of roasted lamb and figs before us, I look at Marcus. "This was better than I ever could've imagined," I say.

He reaches for my hand. "I was thinking the same thing. I love you, Fiona."

"I love you, too," I say, beaming. "Look around us, Marcus. Think of all we've been through with these wonderful people."

The music grows livelier, and Marcus looks at me with a playful grin. "May I have this dance, my wife?"

I smile, nodding as I stand. "I'd be honored." He takes my hand and leads me onto the dance floor.

As we dance together, I feel silly for not knowing the steps, but Marcus helps me along. We stumble our way through, and I can't help but think it's a good metaphor for us—where I feel out of place, he pulls me in, making me feel like I belong.

My life in 2026 feels like a distant memory now. All I left behind was work and a curiosity about history. But now, living in the past, I feel more alive than I ever did in the future. I can't say for certain if I was meant to travel back in time to save Pompeii. Honestly, I often worry about the fact that not everyone heeded our warnings and that I couldn't save everyone. But there's one thing I do know for certain —I was sent back in time to become the wife of Marcus Valerius.

This is our love story, and we're still writing it. We outran Vesuvius together, escaping death. Through the chaos and destruction, we stood side by side, proving that nothing—not even nature's fury—can tear us apart. If we can survive that, then I know our love can endure anything, and with Marcus, I've found my future.

ALSO BY ID JOHNSON

Stand Alone Titles

<u>All I Want for Christmas is Pooch</u>

(*sweet contemporary romance*)

<u>Christmas Memory</u>

(*sweet contemporary romance*)

<u>Meet Cute Me Under the Mistletoe</u>

(*sweet contemporary romance*)

<u>The Doll Maker's Daughter at Christmas</u>

(*clean romance/historical*)

<u>Pretty Little Monster</u>

(*young adult/suspense*)

<u>The Journey to Normal: Our Family's Life with Autism</u> (*nonfiction*)

<u>Found by the Alpha</u> (*fantasy romance*)

Sweet As Maple Syrup series

Leaving Autumn

Cold Turkey

Snowed Inn

Love Throughout Time

(*time travel romance*)

Back to Titanic (free!)

Back to Gettysburg

Back to Bunker Hill

Back to the Highlands

Back to Port Royal

Back to the Inquisition

Back to Salem

Back to Plymouth

Back to Whitechapel

Back to the Old West

Back to the Ton

Back to the Crown

Back to Pompeii

Silverwood Academy

(paranormal romance)

Vampire Hunter (free!)

World Builder

Realm Jumper

Celestial Springs

(psychological thriller/literary fiction/women's fiction)

Beneath the Inconstant Moon

The First Mrs. Edwards

Leaving Ginny

The Motherhood

(dystopian romance)

Rain's Rebellion (free!)

Rain's Run

Rain's Return

Ashes and Rose Petals

(contemporary romance/retelling of Romeo and Juliet and Cinderella)

Girl in the Attic (free!)

Girl From the Tomb

<u>Girl On the Beach</u>

Nashville Country Dreams

(contemporary romance)

<u>Meant to Marry Me (free!)</u>

<u>Lead Me Home</u>

<u>You Are the Reason</u>

Forever Love series

(clean romance/historical)

<u>Cordia's Will: A Civil War Story of Love and Loss</u>

<u>Cordia's Hope: A Story of Love on the Frontier</u>

The Clandestine Saga series

(paranormal romance)

<u>Transformation (free!)</u>

<u>Resurrection</u>

<u>Repercussion</u>

<u>Absolution</u>

<u>Illumination</u>

<u>Destruction</u>

<u>Annihilation</u>

<u>Obliteration</u>

<u>Termination</u>

A Vampire Hunter's Tale (based on The Clandestine Saga)

(paranormal/alternate history)

<u>Aaron (free!)</u>

<u>Jamie</u>

<u>Elliott</u>

<u>Christian</u>

The Chronicles of Cassidy (based on The Clandestine Saga)

(young adult paranormal)

So You Think Your Sister's a Vampire Hunter? (free!)

Who Wants to Be a Vampire Hunter?

How Not to Be a Vampire Hunter

My Life As a Teenage Vampire Hunter

Vampire Hunting Isn't for Morons

Vampires Bite and Other Life Lessons

Gone Guardian

Death Does Not Become Her

Blood of the Vampire Hunter (based on The Clandestine Saga)

(paranormal romance)

Night Slayer (free!)

Shadow Stalker

Queen Catcher

Mother Hunter

Father Finder

Ghosts of Southampton series

(historical romance)

Prelude

Titanic

Residuum

Lusitania

Heartwarming Holidays Sweet Romance series

(Christian/clean romance)

Melody's Christmas (free!)

Christmas Cocoa

Winter Woods

Waiting On Love

Shamrock Hearts

A Blossoming Spring Romance

Firecracker!

Falling in Love

Thankful for You

Melody's Christmas Wedding

The New Year's Date

Charles Town Brides (based on Heartwarming Holidays Sweet Romance)

(Christian/clean romance)

From This Moment (free!)

Can't Help Falling in Love

It's Your Love

When You Say Nothing At All

My Girl

Unchained Melody

I Only Have Eyes For You

At Last

The Very Thought of You

Reaper's Hollow

(paranormal/urban fantasy)

Ruin's Lot (free!)

Ruin's Promise

Ruin's Legacy

When Kings Collide

(steamy historical romance)

Princess of Silence

Princess of Hearts

Collections

Ghosts of Southampton Books 0-2

Reaper's Hollow Books 1-3

The Clandestine Saga Books 1-3

The Chronicles of Cassidy Books 1-4

Celestial Springs Collection

Heartwarming Holidays Sweet Romance Books 1-3

Heartwarming Holidays Sweet Romance Books 4-7

Websites: https://idjohnsonwriter.com/

Follow us on TikTok: @roguewolfpublishing

Follow on Twitter @authoridjohnson

Find me on Facebook at www.facebook.com/IDJohnsonAuthor

Instagram: @authoridjohnson

Follow me on Bookbub: https://www.bookbub.com/authors/id-johnson